BBC
DOCTOR WHO

Royal Blood

BBC

DOCTOR WHO

Royal Blood

Una McCormack

B\D\W\Y
BROADWAY BOOKS
NEW YORK

Copyright © 2015 by Una McCormack

All rights reserved.
Published in the United States by Broadway Books,
an imprint of the Crown Publishing Group,
a division of Penguin Random House LLC, New York.
www.crownpublishing.com

BROADWAY BOOKS and its logo, B\D\W\Y, are trademarks of
Penguin Random House LLC.

This edition published by arrangement with BBC Books, an imprint of
Ebury Publishing, a division of the Random House Group Ltd.

Doctor Who is a BBC Wales production for BBC One. Executive producers:
Steven Moffat and Brian Minchin.

BBC, DOCTOR WHO, AND TARDIS (word marks, logos and devices)
are trademarks of the British Broadcasting Corporation and are used
under license.

Library of Congress Cataloging-in-Publication Data is available upon request

ISBN 978-1-101-90583-8
eBook ISBN 978-1-101-90584-5

Printed in the United States of America

Editorial director: Albert DePetrillo
Series consultant: Justin Richards
Project editor: Steve Tribe
Cover design: Lee Binding © Woodlands Books Ltd 2015
Production: Alex Goddard

2 4 6 8 10 9 7 5 3 1

First U.S. Edition

To Matthew and Verity

Chapter

I

Varuz is lost now. Even the name has gone. The maps have been overwritten; the books burned or locked away in some forgotten library; the children taught different stories in a different tongue. Perhaps high up in the mountains some old goatherd remains, muttering away, his accent thick and impenetrable, with only his charges and the silent peaks to hear him.

We spoke the old language, of course, my wife and I, but only when we were alone together. We told the old tales and sang the old songs, and we took some comfort from them. When the world that you have loved is lost, you hold whatever fragments remain to you, and they are more precious and dear to you than all the riches of the new world. We grieved our loss, and we remembered our past, but in all our long years together, we never spoke of returning. Why would we? In the early days, a return would have brought Conrad's men down upon us and, later, when the long years had made those old struggles meaningless, we knew that the land we had loved was gone for good. We consoled ourselves with the knowledge that it was only in leaving our home that we were able to become husband and wife. Time changes all things; all love ends in one way or another. Only memory remains.

Even my name is different now. To the woman who washes and cleans for me, I am the old man, to be fussed over and reprimanded. To the children who come every other day, I am Grandfather, to be teased and hugged, and have treats coaxed from me. And to those people who come to hear my counsel – the lost and the lonely, the man who can find no love, the woman who can find no rest – I am Father, the holy man, the man of wisdom, the man of peace. To my wife, I was beloved, but those days too are now behind me. And once upon a time, my name was Bernhardt – Lord Bernhardt of Varuz, the land between the mountains and the sea. The lost land. The land that has gone…

Once, they dreamt of glory. Once they dreamt that their names would go down in song and story, appear in lights, that they and their quest would never be forgotten…

They have been travelling for a long time now. When they first set out, they rode on horseback. Now they fly between the stars. Aeons have passed since they set out, and they have been travelling for so long now that they have forgotten their names and their histories. Over the years they have taken on new names and histories, again and again, and forgotten these in turn, again and again… Now they are too old to care about names, or histories. They are too old even to care for glory. All that matters is the quest, whatever that might mean. For they have forgotten even that. There is only the chase, the never-ending chase…

'Are we lost?' Clara peered down into the deep narrow valley. It was very beautiful, she had to admit, with the bright green grass and light dusting of mountain flowers. A touch Heidi. But it wasn't the quasi-mediaeval city she had been promised. It was nothing like a city at all.

'Lost?' The Doctor waved the sonic screwdriver around in an apparently random fashion. 'Of course we're not lost. Lost is a state of mind. Lost is an attitude towards one's circumstances—'

'We *are* lost.'

'Maybe a little.'

'But all we really need is a change of attitude.'

'That,' said the Doctor, 'would be a start.'

Clara smiled to herself. 'There's a path over there,' she said. 'Looks, um, muddy. But it's definitely a path. Why don't we bring some attitude to that?'

The Doctor shrugged. 'As long as it's going down.'

It was indeed going down, and precipitously, but they met the challenge with equanimity and, even, Clara thought, with attitude. When they were back on more level ground, the sun was beginning to set. 'What would happen,' Clara said, asking a question which had been troubling her ever since they had arrived on this world, 'if the TARDIS fell off its perch?' They'd materialised on a very steep slope. There had been some considerable manoeuvring to get out. 'Would it break?'

'Break?' The Doctor stopped mid-step. 'The TARDIS is a highly sophisticated machine. It's practically alive. Do you think it would just let itself fall off a hill?'

Clara reached out a hand to stop the Doctor from taking a tumble himself. 'In fairness, I think we can call this a mountain,' said Clara. 'And there's a thing we call gravity.'

'It wouldn't do too much damage,' said the Doctor, putting both feet firmly down again. 'It never has in the past.'

'Oh good,' said Clara. 'That's encouraging. Next question – and you don't know how I've longed to ask this ever since I took up teaching and got stuck with daytrip duty – are we there yet?'

'Nearly.'

'Nearly. I'll hold you to that. I mean, I'm enjoying the quiet and everything – don't get me wrong – you don't ever really hear quiet, do you? There's always music playing, or someone trying to talk to you, or else the hum of an ancient and precariously balanced time machine. So some silence is nice. But I'm nearly up to my limit. Nearly.'

The Doctor smiled and walked on. Clara followed. The path curved round the mountainside, and, reaching the other side, Clara stopped in her tracks and gasped.

There was a city in the valley – small but grand, with strong square buildings made of a fine yellow stone. A river ran through the city, crossed by – Clara counted – seven iron bridges. Beyond the city lay the sea, over which the sun was setting in a great red ball of flame, glittering orange on the sea and the river, and setting the stone of the city's buildings ablaze.

'Wow,' said Clara.

'Yes,' said the Doctor.

They stood together, in silence, and watched the

darkness gather. The sun slid down the sky, more quickly than one would have expected, until at last it slipped down below the horizon. And then, to Clara's surprise, the city came alight again: bright pricks of yellow light coming from the buildings; strings of light like beads marking out the river.

'Hang on a minute,' said Clara, 'That's electric light! Doctor, I thought we were somewhere olde worlde. Should there be electric lights?'

'Why not?' said the Doctor. 'History can be complicated.'

They admired the pretty cityscape for a while until, suddenly, half the city was plunged into darkness, as if a great blanket had fallen from the sky, smothering out the lights. 'What was that?' said Clara. 'Power cut?'

'Could be,' the Doctor said. His sonic screwdriver was back out, Clara noticed.

She narrowed her eyes. 'Is there something going on here, Doctor?'

'Going on?'

'I don't really believe that you ever go anywhere by chance.'

He gave her a hurt look. 'Now, Clara, that's not entirely fair.'

'No?'

'I'll admit the TARDIS has a knack of finding

places experiencing… how shall we put it? A little local difficulty.'

'Oh, and you love a little local difficulty, don't you, Doctor?'

He gave a mirthless grin. 'Well, it wouldn't be polite to walk on by.'

'Polite?' Clara laughed, as they went on down the slope into the valley. 'When did you get concerned with manners? Anyway, that's not what's I'm really interested in. How come there's electric light down there and nothing proper?'

'Proper?' The Doctor snorted. 'You mean cars, don't you?'

'Not necessarily,' said Clara, although right now she would quite happily have called a local taxi firm to pick them up and take them into town. It was getting chilly.

'You do mean cars,' he said. 'And digital watches.'

'Cars I'll grant you,' said Clara, 'but I really don't mean digital watches.'

But the Doctor was already under way. 'Some civilisations, Clara,' he said, 'understand that technology doesn't have to be about conspicuous consumption. Some civilisations understand that technology is there for no better reason than to make life easier. Technology should *serve* its makers, not make them its servants. Technology isn't something you *have* to have. It isn't something to chase.'

'I swear to you,' Clara said, 'that I have never, in my life, chased after a digital watch. I may once or twice have run for a bus—'

'Some civilisations – *naming no names* – get obsessed with having the latest gadget, the latest app. But other civilisations have more sense. Their technology doesn't control them in the same way. They *make*,' he concluded, 'only what they *need*.'

'Really?' Clara looked down at the city, where the dark quarter remained unlit. 'I bet there's something else they want. Something they'd chase, given the chance.'

In the vast empty reaches of space, there are many places where a person can hide, and many places where objects of great desire can be hidden. Distance and time can make everything disappear – that, and a little cunning. Some things can remain lost for ever, until all memory of them has gone.

But the universe is busy too, busy with curious people who like to find things out, and some people make it their quest to discover what is lost. The traveller aboard this particular ship was exactly that kind of person. He was a collector – a finder of things. He was not a fortune hunter – no, he did not like being described that way; he was not interested in wealth, he said. He was interested in knowledge. What he hated most of all was a hole – a gap in his knowledge. What he hated most of all was that something might exist beyond his ability to see it, to touch it, and to learn from it. He had the best of motives or, at least, his motives were not harmful, which sometimes is as good as it gets.

He has been travelling for a long time, this traveller-collector, and he has visited many different worlds and cultures. While these are not his particular area of interest he has, by necessity, become good at making first contact in a way that does not alarm the locals. When his lead brings him to a new world, he does not hurry down. He takes his time to do his research. He makes sure about the basics, of course – whether he can breathe the air and drink the water (if either of these things exist). He checks for life signs. He checks for intelligent life signs. He checks whether their intelligence has been perverted into belligerence. And, most of all, he tries to find out what these intelligences can do: what they make, what they build, what they craft. He checks for communications technologies. If they are advanced enough, he watches their news and their sports and their entertainments. He may take a little peek into their private communications. (He has blushed, sometimes, at this stage.)

The world he has come to now interests him. There are communications, but they are few and far between, and very irregular. A civilisation on the verge of technological explosion? He studies a little more, and finds the traces of ancient messages in the ether, and comes to a different conclusion. This is a world that was busier, once upon a time, but has now become quiet. That makes his life a little trickier, since now he must find different ways to learn about their culture, but his resources are good, and he is a committed researcher. He is on the trail of something special, something remarkable, and he is working very hard to achieve the object of his desire.

And when he is satisfied that he has done all that he can, his small ship slips quietly down from orbit to land upon a world unfamiliar to the traveller, but which is known now to us. The traveller has followed a trail, and extrapolated a destination, and this leads him to land somewhere between the mountains and the sea…

By the time Clara and the Doctor reached the city it was fully dark, but the road leading towards the gates was lined with great lampposts, ornate and beautifully wrought, and the light from these was enough to make the journey clear. Still, every third or fourth one was not working, and, close up, Clara could see that the iron of the lampposts was flaking away. She saw that the city walls, when she looked closely, were crumbling too, with much loose mortar and worn stone. The gates stood open and were unguarded, and they passed into a great court, cobbled underfoot, and busy with townspeople. Some of these stopped to look at them.

'Aren't city gates usually locked after dark?' said Clara.

'Only if the residents are expecting enemies any moment,' said the Doctor. 'Do we look like enemies?'

'I think we must look like something,' Clara said, as more and more of the townspeople turned to look at them, nudging each other, whispering, sending the news on ahead. 'They probably think we've come to nick the Crown Jewels or something.'

'I have a feeling the Crown Jewels have been sold off some time ago,' muttered the Doctor, running his hand along the old bricks of a wall.

They walked on across the courtyard, a small crowd following them at a slight distance, buzzing with gossip. A narrow street opened before them. 'Up here?' said Clara.

'Why not?' said the Doctor,

He led the way, but they did not get very far. The breadth of the street was blocked by a group of six soldiers, smartly if garishly uniformed, and heading their way.

'Well,' said the Doctor, 'news of our arrival has certainly been passed upstairs quickly. What does that tell us, Clara?'

'That… electric lights might not be the only gizmos they have around here?'

'Spot on. So –' the Doctor turned to face the soldiers and smiled – 'let's find out what I'm supposed to have done now.'

The leader of the group stepped forwards. He was a young man wearing a grand uniform covered in brass buttons and various other pieces of paraphernalia, none of which seemed to be making him feel particularly comfortable. 'In the name of the Most Noble Aurelian, Duke of Varuz, I welcome you to our city.'

'A welcome,' said Clara. 'That's good, isn't it? Doctor, isn't that good?'

'Certainly makes for a pleasant change,' the Doctor said, considerably more cautiously. He moved closer to the young man, and tapped one of the brass buttons. 'Do these do anything?'

'I don't think they do anything, Doctor,' Clara said. 'I think they're decoration.'

'Decoration?' The Doctor peered at the button more closely. 'Why? What for?' He tugged at the button which, mercifully, remained in place. Had Clara been in the officer's place, she might have lost her patience, but the young man was staring at the Doctor keenly, almost earnestly. Clara found herself rather taken by him.

'Hope against hope,' the young man said, softly. 'Could this be the change we have been waiting for? Could this be the moment when the tide turns?'

His ruminations got no further. Another of the guard, an older man, grey-haired and with slightly less in the way of decoration, stepped forwards. 'Enough of a delay, eh, my lord? His highness is waiting to receive our visitors.'

The young man stiffened, as if caught out in an indiscretion. 'We're hardly delaying—'

'You know how your uncle doesn't like to be kept waiting.'

The young man flushed scarlet. He turned on his heel and called out to the rest of the company to follow. The older man, smiling, gestured to the Doctor and Clara to follow, and took up position behind them.

'Phew,' said Clara, under her breath. 'How not to win over your boss…'

They passed on further into the city, through streets made narrow by the high square buildings and made only slightly less shadowy under the intermittent glare of lamp-light. They crossed three of the bridges, the river black and slow-moving beneath and, after a good fifteen minutes' walk, came at last to a sturdy palace. Its walls, high and solid, gave it the guarded air of a citadel, although the arched windows and gold and blue mosaics above the great doors made clear that display was at least as important as defence, or had been once upon a time. Now the stonework was as chipped and worn as it was throughout the rest of the city, and the colours of the mosaics had almost faded away.

The great palace doors were guarded by four men in heavy armour. The young officer went ahead to speak to them and Clara, thinking over the young man's words, said suddenly, 'Doctor, have you been here before and forgotten to mention it?'

'What?' The Doctor, who had been playing with some kind of device or other, palming it around in his hand, stopped and put the thing away. 'Not that I remember. Why?'

Clara nodded to the young man, now in quiet

conversation with the palace guards. 'I thought that maybe he had recognised you.'

The Doctor shrugged. 'I suppose I might come here next.'

Clara sighed. 'What does that even *mean*?'

'It's perfectly straightforward—'

'It's all right. Really. I get it.' She nodded at the guards. 'Look, they've got swords. That's not very high-tech.'

'Look again, Clara,' the Doctor said softly.

She peered at them. 'I am looking again. Long thin things, presumably pointy and sharp inside those jackets.'

'Those "jackets" are actually "scabbards".'

'Mm, I think I prefer "jackets". Keeps them cosy. What am I missing?'

'Plenty, I should think.' The Doctor smiled. 'But those swords? They aren't metal, for one thing.'

'No?' Clara stared at them more closely. Long, thin, pointy…

'No,' said the Doctor. 'I think they're lasers.'

'Really? Like light sabres?' Clara was impressed. 'That could actually be quite brilliant.'

'Not if you're on the receiving end. We'll try not to test them, yes?'

'You're the boss.'

The young man, finishing his conversation with

the guards, gestured to them to follow. As they walked towards the palace doors, the guards fell back, saluting them as they passed through.

Clara said, 'You're *quite* sure you haven't been here?'

'Yes!'

'It's just everyone seems to be showing you a great deal of respect…' Clara laughed. 'Oh, hang on, now I *do* believe you haven't been here before.'

Inside, the building had the same air of faded glamour; the great arched windows had cracks and chips in the small panes of glass; many of the tiles underfoot were broken; and the gold worked into the walls was peeling away or completely gone. They came to another guarded doorway, and the young lord went ahead to speak to the guards. The older officer followed him, much to the young man's clear irritation.

'Is it me,' said Clara, 'or does everything look like it's falling down? I don't mean in a Michael Douglas way—'

Suddenly, the young man lost his temper. He banged the flat of his hand against the wall.

'Or perhaps I do,' said Clara thoughtfully. The older officer came back towards them, but Clara watched as the young man got himself under control. When the older man reached them again,

Clara said, 'Your boss doesn't seem happy.'

The soldier smiled. 'The young lord? Oh, Lord Mikhail's not happy about anything.'

'Probably doesn't like you muscling in all the time.'

'Clara,' said the Doctor, 'let's leave this for the moment.' He turned to the officer. 'I assume you're taking us to the Duke?'

'Where else? You're expected. Have been for some time.'

The young man, now fully under control again – in fact, if anything, a little too stiff, led them through the doors into the hall.

'"Expected for some time?"' Clara frowned. 'Doctor, you're absolutely sure this place is new to you and you're new to them?'

The Doctor looked uncomfortable. 'I think so… There've been a lot of places.'

Clara sighed. 'I bet you my digital watch we'll be seeing the inside of the dungeons within the hour.'

As they passed into the hall, they were announced. *The ambassador and his servant!*

'"*Ambassador*"?' said Clara. 'Give me a break!'

But the Doctor had the trump card. He burst out laughing. '"*Servant*"?'

For months at a time they can exist in silence, doing no

23

more than what is necessary to keep them going. To keep them searching, searching… for something they can barely remember. They have forgotten what. They have forgotten why. There is only a single word…

And then, suddenly, the instrumentation springs into life. Lights flash. Alarms sound. A sighting! A reading! A trace! A tiny chance that here, in this new place that they have never visited before, they will find some answers. They will discover the object of their quest…

The universe is vast, and holds many secrets. They could search for ever, and they will. But today, they have come to this particular world, and on that world they have a particular destination. They are coming to the land that lies between the mountains and the sea…

I have thought many times, over the years, of writing down what happened in those last days. At first, I would not have dared – it would have given us away, if found, but, later, I always came back to the same difficulty: who would read such a history? Who would care to read about the end of a lost and unlamented land, written in a lost unspoken tongue?

I am old. There is nobody in this world to whom I could speak who would understand. Conrad is long dead; the young lord is gone. I am the last, unless those strange wanderers who passed through Varuz in those last days remember something of us yet. But when I think of them, and reflect upon them, it seems to me that they were cloaked in a kind of deliberate forgetfulness, as if their pasts were not to be admitted, keeping them mindful of nothing more than the present… Do they remember? No, I am not convinced that they remember. I am not convinced that they remember us at all, or, if they do, we are only part of a succession of adventures and rapidly passing events, that merge like ripples on a stream. Only I remain constant, it seems, with my memories, which are now fading. The days pass, and I feel my strength slipping away from me. And I find that I must write down what happened – for myself, so that I can leave this world knowing that some record survives me of those days. Perhaps one day, somebody will find it. Perhaps the secrets of an unknown script will intrigue them, and they will seek to decipher what I have written. Perhaps my story will move them. Perhaps, for the brief time that they give me their attention, Varuz will live again, as it was once; or as it could have been. As my memory has made it.

I take heart from this. So I will write down all that happened, in those strange last days that followed after the holy man came to Varuz…

Chapter

2

The hall into which they had been brought was high-ceilinged and many-pillared, and, at the far end, was a slightly raised dais upon which two plain black seats had been placed. A man sat on one of these, and a woman on the other. Both of them were richly dressed. Slightly to one side, and a step or two down from them, was another man, dressed all in black. The young officer, Lord Mikhail, gestured to Clara and the Doctor to follow him down the hall towards the trio.

Their footsteps echoed on the stone flags, and Clara was very conscious of the eyes of the three people upon them. 'Nice digs,' she said to Mikhail.

'The Great Hall,' the Doctor said, grandly.

'You're still absolutely sure that you've not been here before?'

'Well, what else is it going to be called?' said

the Doctor. 'It's never the Mediocre Hall or the In Urgent Need of Renovation Hall. It's always the Great Hall. Although looking round this one…'

'A lick of paint wouldn't do any harm,' Clara agreed.

When they reached the dais, Mikhail bowed and said, 'My lord Duke; my lady Duchess. Your guests.'

Clara glanced between Mikhail and the woman. Up close, the similarity between him and the woman was clear: his dark hair was military-short and hers was long and held in place beneath a jewelled cap, but both had golden tints that glinted in the light. His long fingers were curled around the hilt of his sword; hers, ring-encrusted, sat twined upon her lap. They were obviously related – but how? Clara wasn't exactly getting parental vibes.

Mikhail, turning to the Duke, said, 'My lord—'

But the Duke lifted his hand to stop the young man from speaking. 'We thank you for your service in bringing our guests, Lord Mikhail,' he said. 'You may leave us now.'

The young man hesitated. He clearly wanted to be present throughout the following encounter, and he glanced over at the Duchess, as if looking for support. Almost imperceptibly, she shook her head. The scarlet flush passed over Mikhail's face again, but he bowed, turned, and left.

'Families, huh?' said Clara, to nobody in particular.

The Duke, frostily, replied, 'Lord Mikhail has a strong will. A flaw in many young men.'

'It's not really any of my business,' Clara said. 'But he seems to mean well.'

The Duke, however, had turned his attention to the Doctor. 'I am Aurelian,' he said, 'Duke of the Most Ancient, Serene, and Noble State of Varuz.' He reached out to rest his left hand upon the arm of the woman next to him. 'My wife, the Duchess Guena.' He nodded to the man standing beside him. 'And the Lord Bernhardt.'

In the silence that followed, Clara studied each them in turn. The Duke was fortyish, square and strong and obvious. His wife was about the same age, all the more beautiful for the small lines around her mouth and eyes, which were sharp and intelligent. Bernhardt was so undistinguished as to be practically part of the shadows. Clara was impressed. She imagined he must put a lot of effort into doing that.

The pause continued. 'What are they waiting for?' whispered Clara.

'Search me,' the Doctor whispered back, then, clearing his throat, he said, 'Sorry, was I meant to be saying something at this point?' He waved at them. 'Hello yourselves!' Then he frowned. 'Was that meant to be more formal?'

Bernhardt stepped forward and studied them both closely. Then he turned back to the Duke. 'My lord,' he said quietly, 'this is not the ambassador.'

'No,' said the Doctor, 'I'm not an ambassador. Well… No, let's not complicate things. I'm not any ambassador you're expecting. Probably. No, not probably. Not at all.'

Bernhardt glanced behind them and Clara became conscious that there were people moving in softly. 'Doctor,' she murmured, 'light sabres at seven o'clock.'

Quietly, Bernhardt said, 'So who are you?'

'Doctor,' Clara said, more urgently, 'they're getting closer—'

'All right—'

'If you've been here before and insulted people, I'll take a laser to you myself—'

'Calm down, Clara—'

'So start apologising, or something. Anything. *Now!*'

'I come in peace!' cried the Doctor.

Aurelian lifted his hand. The guards – and their lasers – got no closer. Slowly, Aurelian rose from his chair. In wonder, he said, 'I know you. I know who you are.' Stepping down from the dais, he walked towards the Doctor and then knelt before him. The Doctor gave an embarrassed laugh.

'You're loving this, aren't you?' said Clara.

The Doctor patted Aurelian awkwardly on the shoulder. 'You know, I don't think this is entirely necessary…'

But the Duke's head was bowed. 'We are honoured by your arrival,' he said. 'Honoured that you have made the long and difficult journey in such dark times to come to us. Please,' he said, standing, and clasping the Doctor's hand in his own, 'take my seat. You are most welcome here. All I ask for – if I may – is your counsel.'

The Doctor made himself comfortable in the chair. 'Well, for starters, I think you should keep an eye on that young man. Who is he? He's not your son, is he?' He looked from Duke to Duchess. 'A nephew, I bet. You didn't pinch his throne did you? That never turns out well. Before you know it everyone's been poisoned—'

'Doctor,' said Clara. 'We're doing so well.'

Bernhardt stepped forwards. 'My lord,' he said, 'you have the advantage. Who is this man?'

Aurelian, rising from his feet, turned to Bernhardt. His eyes were shining. 'Don't you see, Bernhardt? He is a wanderer, a pilgrim.'

31

'He's got you down,' said Clara.

Guena look down at her husband. 'A holy man?'

'Or perhaps not,' Clara concluded.

The Doctor shrugged. 'A holy man?' he said to himself. 'I can run with that.'

Aurelian reached out to clasp the Doctor's hand. 'I cannot think when one of your kind last came to us here beyond the mountains!'

'Not in my father's time,' said Guena. She was looking at the Doctor with what Clara could only call 'suspicion', and Bernhardt, too, seemed less than convinced. 'The last duke was my father. He would have told me if a holy man had come our way, before my birth.'

'The path through the mountains is not easily taken these days,' Bernhardt said. 'How did you find your way across?'

The Doctor tapped his forehead. 'Oh, you know. Excellent sense of direction.'

Clara watched Guena and Bernhardt exchange a look. But Aurelian was completely enamoured. 'We must speak,' he said. 'Dark days are upon us—'

Suddenly, in a rustle of silks, the Duchess stood. Turning to Clara, she said, 'Come. Let us leave the men to their talk.'

Clara frowned. 'I think I'll stay, if it's all the same to you.'

Guena held out her hand, heavy with numerous spectacularly ornate rings that looked like they weren't going to take 'no' for an answer. 'Come.'

Clara turned to the Doctor, who jerked his head. *Go on, do your thing.*

'Oh, for pity's sake,' muttered Clara. With a deep sense of grievance, she followed the Duchess away from the Great Hall, and the discussion that was about to happen.

A holy man? I did not believe it then, and I do not believe it now. In my wanderings since we left Varuz I have met men that could indeed be called 'holy'; men with such capacity for serenity that simply to be with them was to wash one's spirit clean. This was not such a man. This man burned like fire. Yes, fire might purify, but that was not the kind of peace that we desired. I did not doubt that this was a remarkable man; no, not for one moment did I doubt that. But holy? No. Was he a man of wisdom? Certainly, for long life and rich experience and a sharp mind upon which to reflect upon these experiences constitute wisdom. Certainly this was such a man. But this man was a maelstrom. And Aurelian, of course, wished above all for him to give his blessing to whatever ventures he might divine.

Poor Aurelian…

I should speak, perhaps, of Aurelian, the last Duke of Varuz, since there is no one else who remembers him now, and I shall try to be fair, for he was not an evil man – no, not by any means, but a desperate man, and one who set himself upon a course of action that could not succeed. In a different time, perhaps, or without the burden of rule, he would surely have been remembered as fearless and strong, a great hero. He was all these things throughout his life. But the times were not his. The times required compromise, humility, sacrifice – and these were by no means Aurelian's gifts. I do not mean to say that I possessed these qualities, for all of us were proud during those times, and desired more than we could ever have. No, it was not all Aurelian's fault. Guena was too proud, and I was insufficiently wise. We all of us were the wrong people, at the wrong time, and it seemed to us – to my wife and me – that all we could do was choose between the lesser of two defeats.

When the women departed to talk about their own business, we too left the Great Hall. Aurelian, leading, took us to an antechamber beside the Hall where he kept his maps and made his plans and dreamed his dreams of a country brought back to glory. Here, he showed our visitor – the Doctor, he called himself – the land between the mountains and the sea. Here were the high passes, which Conrad's scouts now controlled; and here the waterways, which Conrad's ships now controlled. And here was all that remained under our jurisdiction: the rough wild country to the north; the empty plains, which had once been rich farmland, to the south. The few small towns and villages. And the river and the city, our last stronghold.

'This must have been a beautiful country once,' the Doctor said. 'But even from my short time here I can see that all is not well.'

Aurelian was grieved; indeed, we were all grieved to see our land crumbling in our care.

'We struggle,' I said. 'All across the land the people struggle. Once, we were rich, yes. But these days we are poor.'

Aurelian's eyes were flashing. 'Aye, and we all know who to blame!' He pointed on the map to the land beyond the mountains. 'We are besieged!'

'Besieged?' The Doctor thick eyebrows rose for a moment; then he turned his attention back to the map, where Aurelian had pointed. 'So what's over there?' he said. 'Beyond the mountains? Who's besieging you?'

'Conrad,' Aurelian said. 'That is Conrad's country. From there, he rules almost the whole world.'

'Almost?' said the Doctor.

Aurelian smiled. 'Except for Varuz. He does not rule the land between the mountains and the sea. But he seeks to conquer us.'

'Conrad has a great strength in arms,' I explained, pointing to the mountain passes. 'His men patrol the borders. They prevent entrance, and exit, into Varuz.'

The Doctor stared at the map. 'And he's hoping… What? To starve you out?'

'The winter is over again without him succeeding in that aim,' I said. 'Summer is coming, and we may feed ourselves from the land a little longer. My thinking is that Conrad will not wait for another winter. He will enter Varuz with the good weather.'

The Doctor gave me a very sharp look. 'You know this for sure?'

'I conjecture,' I said.

'Conjecture, eh?' He stared back down at the map. 'So what do you want from a holy man? What do you want from me?'

Aurelian gave his broad and handsome smile. 'What do I want? I want your blessing, of course!'

The Doctor looked at him uneasily. 'My blessing?'

'On my endeavours.'

'Your endeavours.' Slowly, the Doctor walked round the map, as if taking in every pebble on the mountain paths, every blade of green grass in the valleys, every ruined villa and every lost village. 'Endeavours. You mean war, don't you?'

'Is that so terrible a thing?' said Aurelian.

'Yes,' said the Doctor.

'Even in the name of peace?'

The Doctor almost spat. 'That's nonsense. Double speak. *Lies*—'

For a moment I thought Aurelian might become angry, but then I saw a glistening of water in his eyes. To see a proud man weep and to be unable to help it is a dreadful thing. Softly, Aurelian said, 'Good father, we are beleaguered. Conrad's ambition is without limit. He wants to push us into the sea – drown us, obliterate us. He wants Varuz for his own. He wants the *world* for his own.'

I was watching our visitor very carefully now, and, for a while, I must admit that I was afraid. He did not seem to me the kind of man to bow down to tyrants, to submit to superior force, and it seemed that Aurelian's words had stirred something within him, some great deep anger.

'My people waver,' Aurelian said. 'My knights and my lords – they waver too.' He turned to me and, with a smile, clasped my hand. 'Not you, Bernhardt. Never you. But the others? I know they are afraid.' He turned back to the Doctor. 'With your blessing, good father, we might find our resolve once more. We might pull together and make one more stand in the mountains. Conrad is coming, so Bernhardt says – but we can deny him! We can show him that Varuz can never be taken. Perhaps –' his face was shining now – 'this might be the start of a new age for Varuz. With Conrad dismissed, we could begin to heal ourselves – become whole again. Restore the glamour and glory that we had here, once upon a time…'

Dreams and delusions. Castles in the air. The wrong man, at the wrong time. I saw the Doctor watching me, and I had to turn away – in shame? In shame. It is a cruel thing to know that one's home is on its knees.

When the Doctor spoke again, he spoke firmly, but with compassion. 'War is a terrible thing,' he said. 'I know. You talk about a stand, Aurelian, but it would be a massacre. There's no honour in self-sacrifice, and no honour in sacrificing others with you, throwing away lives in a battle that can't be won…'

He hesitated here, and I wondered what this

man's experience of war had been. What a warrior he would have made, it seemed to me, had war ever been his business.

'A holy man,' the Doctor said, 'a *truly* holy man – would try to make peace. Conrad's ambassador is on his way still, I assume. So my advice is – accept the embassy. Talk to Conrad's representative. See if there's still a chance to make peace. See on what terms he might allow you to continue in peace here, beyond the mountains.'

Poor Aurelian. That was not what he wanted to hear. But it was the truth. It was what I had been trying to tell him since he had taken upon the dukedom all those years ago, after I had seen at first-hand Conrad's country, his knights and his weaponry. Our poor horses, even our laser-swords, were nothing to what Conrad had at his disposal. There could be no glorious victory, but neither could we be allowed to remain as we were, on the edge, proof of the limits of Conrad's rule. We were old, and proud, and, yes, crafty in many ways, but these would never be enough. Our task was to carry what we could through these times, and to hope that not everything was destroyed. Or so I understood at the time.

'If the ambassador is coming,' said the Doctor, 'you should meet him. Hear what he has to say.

Don't underestimate peace, my lord. You'll miss it, when it's gone. When the buildings are burning and the soldiers dying, and the children are ripped from their parents' arms – you'll regret the day you ever went to war.'

I saw then that the Doctor's eye was as much on me as it was on Aurelian. But if he thought I was in need of persuasion, he had misjudged me. I already agreed. But I was willing to put whatever weight I could behind this attempt to sway Aurelian.

'He speaks wisely, my lord,' I said, quietly. 'Let us wait for the ambassador. Let us welcome him. Let us try to make peace.'

'Peace?' said Aurelian. 'Or surrender?' But he clasped my hand again, and I knew that, for the sake of our long friendship, he was still listening.

Clara followed Guena out of the great hall, and along a narrow corridor to a little sitting room. Here, comfortable chairs were arranged around a low table, and small lamps were lit, giving the room a warm, cosy atmosphere. Even the bare patches on the carpets and tapestries added to the effect, making the space feel lived-in and well-loved.

At Guena's invitation, Clara sat in one of the seats, sinking back into the comfortable cushions. Guena rang a little bell and, shortly afterwards, a servant appeared through a side door, carrying a tray laid out with a silver jug and tiny silver cups. When the servant left, Guena poured out the drink, and Clara sipped it. It was thick and hot and sweet, a little like hot chocolate. She watched as, one by one, Guena took off her rings, as if she was a knight stripping herself of her armour. She kept her eyes on Clara throughout, and Clara had the distinct impression of being scrutinised thoroughly – and judged.

She seemed to have no intention of making the first conversational move, however, so Clara decided she might as well be the one to start talking. 'Don't you hate being sent away?'

'Sent away?' Guena looked around. 'You mean in here? Why would I hate that?'

'While the men talk business, I mean.'

'What is to stop us from talking? About whatever we choose?'

Clara laughed. 'Well, nothing, I suppose.'

Guena smiled back. 'Nothing.' The smile disappeared as she gave Clara a very sharp look. 'Your master—'

'He's really not that,' said Clara. 'Absolutely not that.'

'Father? Lover?'

'Er, none of the above!' Clara struggled for a

word to describe the Doctor, eventually settling on: 'Friend.'

Guena looked surprised, but accepted the explanation. 'Your friend, then. He's not an ambassador, for sure, but he's not a pilgrim either, is he? He's not a holy man.'

'No, he's not, at least, not in the way you mean,' said Clara. 'But he's a traveller, all right. He's seen a lot, he's done a lot. He's got more experience than I think either of us can imagine. If your husband—'

Guena stiffened slightly. 'The Duke,' she said.

'I'm sorry,' said Clara at once. 'I don't mean to be rude. I'm not used to this kind of thing.'

Guena gave a quick nod to indicate that she accepted the apology.

'What I mean is that if the Duke wants advice, he could definitely do worse than ask the Doctor.' She leaned forwards in her chair. 'So what's going on? You were expecting an ambassador, weren't you? Who from? And why is everything so…' She stopped, unsure how to word her question without seeming rude. How did you say to someone: '*Have you noticed that your city is falling down?*' Chances were that Guena *had* noticed, and that it was causing her some distress.

It was clear that Guena understood. 'Ah, if you could have seen us at our height, Clara! Five hundred years ago, six hundred – what a place this was then! What a country this must have been!' Her eyes shone. 'The whole city, so they say, was bright as daylight, even at night. Great ships sped across the water; great ships flew amongst the clouds. We could speak to each other at great distance – and could be with each in the twinkling of an eye. And we were not a little people trapped in a little land. Our influence stretched far beyond here. Far beyond the mountains, far beyond the seas.'

Clara looked around the faded room and thought of the crumbling city outside. 'Five hundred years is a long time ago.'

'And Varuz is very different now,' said Guena. 'Here we are, trapped behind our mountains, sitting in the gloom behind crumbling walls, and our enemies wait for their moment to come.'

'Your enemies?'

Quickly, Guena explained what Aurelian was, in the next room, explaining to the Doctor: that across the mountains a powerful country, led by Conrad, was poised to invade. 'The passes are closely watched,' Guena said, 'and very few get through. But we have received news to expect an ambassador from Conrad. That is why – when you arrived – we thought that you must be from him. Very few come through the mountains now.'

'But you received news of this ambassador? Who from?'

'Even in Conrad's country there are people who sympathise with our plight,' Guena said, and gave a crafty smile.

'People,' said Clara. 'You mean spies.'

'If you prefer.'

Not much, thought Clara. 'Spies. That young man who brought us here…'

'Lord Mikhail.'

'He doesn't seem very happy. What's going on there?'

Guena contemplated the question for a while. 'Mikhail is ambitious for Varuz. My husband –' so it was OK for Guena to call him that – 'is afraid that this ambition extends as far as the dukedom.'

Clara frowned. 'Your husband sounds paranoid. Sorry, I mean the Duke. The Duke sounds paranoid.' She frowned. 'You know, on reflection, that doesn't sound any less rude.'

But Guena was not angry. 'Not paranoid,' she said. 'No, that is not fair. But it is fair to say that Aurelian is fearful for Varuz, and also fair to say that he is overburdened by his charge. Change is coming to Varuz. We all know that – even Aurelian, in his heart. None of us can stop that.'

'I get the impression the Duke would like to,'

said Clara. 'I get the impression he would turn the clock back, if he could.'

'All of us,' said Guena softly, 'would be glad to see Varuz as it was once. Instead…' She looked around them. 'Instead, we have inherited what you see.'

'Something's going to give,' said Clara.

'Change does not have to mean devastation,' said Guena. 'But the people are tired. They are afraid. They want peace, Clara. We all want peace. We don't want to suffer any longer.'

Clara studied the Duchess thoughtfully. 'Why are you telling me all this?'

Guena leaned in and spoke more softly. 'Conrad's ambassador is coming. I am sure of it.'

'And?'

'And,' said the Duchess, 'I may need someone to speak for me.'

Not speak for Aurelian, Clara thought, and then she remembered something Guena had said: *The last duke was my father*. Guena had wasted no time in taking her away to talk in private. Who, Clara wondered, was really running the show here? Who, really, was in charge? Aurelian was the warrior, yes, but was Guena the schemer? And what did that make Bernhardt?

'We are not strong,' said Guena. 'These days we

are a quiet country, on the very edge of the world. Our glory days are long behind us, and we cannot defend ourselves, not against the army that Conrad commands. The question now is whether anything of Varuz will survive the coming days. Clara,' she urged, 'open war will destroy us completely. If the ambassador comes – will you help me? Will you help Varuz?'

Slowly, Clara said, 'I can't make any promises.'

Guena smiled. 'I don't want promises. I want help. When the time comes.'

'Then let's see,' said Clara. 'When the time comes.'

Chapter

3

The guest quarters that were assigned to them had the same threadbare cosiness as Guena's sitting room. There was a big shared room, set off from which Clara found two bedchambers, each one plain but clean, with a huge bed and many soft pillows and coverings.

Clara set herself to exploring all the chests and cupboards, and was delighted to find that one was full of fine dresses. She spent a happy half-hour choosing one to wear, trying them for size and fit and colour, settling at last on a deep red gown with a full skirt and much rich brocade worked into the bodice. It had wide sleeves, cut from a dark orange cloth and covered in golden embroidery and small jewels. She stretched out her arms, admiring the butterfly wing effect, and luxuriated in the fine, heavy cloth.

'Good idea to have such thick clothes,' she said. 'I imagine it could get cold here. The wind from the mountains in one direction. The wind from the sea in the other. And whatever else is working round here, I'm not sure the central heating is switched on.'

The Doctor too had been prowling the room, stopping here and there to pick up objects and examine them: a vase; a picture; a cup. Clara, spreading out the skirts of her dress, arranged herself on a chaise longue and made herself comfortable. He looked like he would be keeping himself busy like this for a while yet.

'So I talked with the Duke's wife,' she said.

Reaching the window, the Doctor came to a halt.

'It was interesting,' said Clara. '*Really* interesting.'

The Doctor grunted and touched one of the curtains. It too was made from thick cloth, not as fine as her dress, but it was covered in small jewels and crystals. It was very beautiful, but not what Clara wanted the Doctor to be concentrating on right now. He should be concentrating on what she was saying.

'So about the Duchess,' Clara said. 'I think she wants to overthrow the government.'

The Doctor gave another grunt.

'And I've decided I'm going to make my fortune

by selling her guns. Do you know any arms dealers?' This time there was no response at all. Clara was starting to miss the grunting. 'Doctor, are you listening?'

'These *jewels*!' he said.

Clara stared at them. True, they were sparkling nicely in the lamplight, but sparkling nicely in the lamplight was par for the course for jewels. It was what you had jewels for. 'What about them?'

'They're driving me crazy!'

'In what way, Doctor?' Clara said, patiently.

'It's not the sparkling. I can put up with that, even though it's *annoying*. But they don't seem to have a function. Things can't just go around *sparkling*. Nothing round here is wasted! These jewels wouldn't just be,' he spat the word out, '*decoration*.'

'Why not?' Clara lifted up the beautiful sleeves and let them spread out. 'What's wrong with a little decoration?'

'It's frippery.'

'"Frippery"? Who in the world uses a word like that? Who in the *universe*? Anyway, what's the harm in some occasional frippery?'

'It's pointless.'

Clara ran her finger along the beads sewn into her sleeves. 'It's pretty.'

'It's a waste of the finite resources of the universe.'

'Says the man with sparkles on his jumper.'

The Doctor stared down at his jumper as if noticing it for the first time. 'These help me to see in the dark.'

Clara lifted up her arm. 'And these make my right hook extra weighty. Look, Doctor, do you want to hear about the conversation I had with the Duchess or not? We didn't just talk about frocks in there, you know. In fact, we didn't talk about frocks at all.'

The Doctor had turned back to his curtains. 'Go on. If you must.'

'Doctor – I think she's plotting against the Duke.'

The Doctor wasn't particularly perturbed by this news. 'I assumed somebody would be. Where there's a throne, there's a plot.'

'But his own wife?'

'I'm not seeing any contradictions there.'

'Perhaps plot is too strong a word,' Clara said thoughtfully. 'But she wants me to talk to Conrad's ambassador, if he ever arrives.'

'Well,' the Doctor said with a sigh, '*somebody* has to speak to him, and it's not going to be me—'

'Doctor, stop measuring for curtains and listen! She doesn't want me to talk to him officially! She wants me to talk to him in private. Without anyone else knowing. Behind the Duke's back.'

The Doctor dropped the curtains and turned to look at her. 'She wants you to *spy* for her?'

'Oh, now you're listening!' Clara said, with some exasperation. 'No, she didn't ask me to *spy* for her. What do you think I am? She asked me to carry a message for her.'

'Behind the Duke's back. To the representative of his mortal enemy. What do you call that? Because I know what I call it—'

'Doctor,' Clara said seriously, 'I don't know what to do.'

He turned back to the curtains.

'Doctor!'

And then he turned back to her. He looked puzzled, as if he'd thought the conversation had been closed. 'Well, of course you have to do it!'

Clara was startled. 'What? But, isn't that...' She trailed off.

'Isn't it what?'

'Well, *treason*?'

The Doctor gave her a very tricky smile. 'Not technically.'

'Doctor. There are swords. Which are also lasers. And there may be other things. Deathly curtains. I need more than technicalities. Wouldn't spying for the Duchess be treason?'

'Only if you were one of Aurelian's knights or vassals. Which you're not.' He gave her a worried look. 'You're not, are you?

'Let me think,' said Clara. 'What does it say on my passport? Er, no, I think that's something to do with the Queen, or possibly Brussels—'

'You've not gone and accidentally sworn an oath to anyone or anything since we got here, have you?'

'I certainly hope not! Er, how would I know?'

'There's usually a book involved. Sometimes blood.' He gave her a sly look. 'You haven't accepted any drinks, have you?'

'What?' She thought of the nice chocolatey thing she had drunk with Guena.

'I'm joking,' he said.

'Well, don't!'

'So if you're not Aurelian's subject, and you've not sworn an oath, how can it be treachery?'

'You're confusing me!' Clara said, plaintively.

'It's very simple,' said the Doctor. 'You're not from Varuz. Aurelian doesn't *own* you. You can do what you like. Do you *want* to be Guena's messenger girl?'

'You're not making it sound an attractive career choice.'

'Then let me put it this way,' said the Doctor. 'Do

you want to help stop a war?'

'What? Of course!'

The Doctor turned back to his inspection of the curtains. 'If what you've told me about her is true, so does Guena. Aurelian – well, that's less clear.'

Clara frowned. 'The Duke can't really want war. He might want the *idea* of war – but not *actual* war.'

'I'm not so sure. Some people start worrying about their legend far too early,' said the Doctor. 'Worrying about legacy. They want to make sure that they're remembered – but for the right reasons. Aurelian knows as well as anyone else that he can't hold Conrad back. Either he can surrender or he can go down in a blaze of glory. And who wants to be remembered for a surrender?'

Clara shivered, and wrapped the great sleeves of the dress around her. 'That's madness.'

'Yes it is,' said the Doctor. 'But it's *popular* madness. This ambassador, though – if he ever turns up – he might be someone with real power to stop a pointless war happening. And if someone who has connections to people close to the Duke, but no vested interest in the politics of Varuz, passed on a message that Varuz was interested in a peaceful settlement…' He peered at Clara. 'I mean you, by the way, is that clear?'

'As crystal,' said Clara.

'Clara,' he said, 'I want to stop this war. The ambassador might be exactly the person we need, and you might be exactly the person to speak to him.' He waved his hand about. 'But of course, if you're suddenly getting *scruples* about high treason and whatnot… We can't be seen to get our hands dirty, now, can we?'

'All right, all right, you've made your point!'

'A little chat with a visiting dignitary won't do anyone any harm,' the Doctor said firmly.

'I hope not,' said Clara. 'Those lasers look *burny*.'

'It's the right choice.'

'I'm not sure it *feels* right.'

'Cheer up,' said the Doctor. 'It might never happen. We've no idea if this ambassador is really coming.'

He didn't, that night, and Clara slept well in her deep and comfortable bed, despite the thought of lasers. But the morning brought the sound of silver trumpets, and a messenger to their room came to inform them that the Duke requested the presence of his learned friend the holy man, in an audience with the ambassador from Conrad.

'Come along,' the Doctor said to Clara. 'You're bound to find out something useful.'

'Hmm,' said Clara.

'Not convinced?'

'I'm not convinced it'll be the real ambassador this time either,' Clara replied.

'That would be ridiculous,' the Doctor said.

The Doctor and his companion were already with the Duke in his map room when I arrived. Aurelian, I could see, was plainly nervous, pacing around the small space, stopping now and then to examine his maps, as if to remind himself of some minor detail or other. He saw me and smiled, and I nodded and bowed, and took my place in one quiet corner of the room, to remain there until my lord or lady needed me.

At length, Aurelian ceased his prowling, coming to a halt before the Doctor. 'Holy man,' he said, and reached out his hands. 'I am grateful for your presence here today. Is there any wisdom that you would convey to me?'

The Doctor hesitated, but, to my amusement, his young friend nudged him forwards with her elbow, and, with ill grace, he took the Duke's hands and patted them, rather awkwardly. 'Don't go looking for war,' he said. 'But if you look for peace, you will have the gratitude of all your people. And that, Duke, should be your heart's desire.'

Aurelian was soothed by this. He nodded his thanks and released the Doctor's hands. But his quieter, steadier mood was disturbed by the arrival of Mikhail here in his private chamber. I cannot blame the young lord, but his timing could surely not have been worse.

'My lord Duke,' he said, bowing as he made his approach. 'I beg you – no, I must insist – I should be present when the ambassador meets you.'

Aurelian turned to him, eyes sparking with anger. 'Insist, do you?' He looked at me. 'Do you hear that, Bernhardt? The young lord *insists*.'

'My lord,' I said, and stepped forwards. 'Ask yourself – would it do any harm?'

'Any *harm*?' He frowned at me, but we had been friends for many years, and I did not fear his anger on my own account. I was conscious, too, of the Doctor, watching this whole scene unfold, and while I still knew little about him, I did not want to give too much away. 'Aurelian,' I said, gently. I hardly ever used his name, so he knew that it was one of those rare occasions when I presumed to call upon our long friendship, and he paid me the courtesy of listening to me. 'Mikhail would learn a great deal from being present. There is much to be gained and nothing to be lost.'

Aurelian gave a great sigh, but I could see his anger had passed. 'Very well. The boy can stay.' Mikhail was clearly not pleased to be called such a name, but I gestured to him to be quiet, and to accept that he had what he wanted, and he had the good sense to obey.

Then a messenger came to say that the ambassador was approaching the Hall, and Aurelian prepared himself for the meeting. 'Holy man,' he said, appealing to the Doctor, 'will you give me your blessing?'

'Look for peace, my lord,' the Doctor urged again.

'I will not surrender,' said Aurelian.

The Doctor did not reply, but I could see in his face his thoughts: *You might not have a choice.* And I had not failed to notice that any blessing that could have been given had been withheld.

Leaving the antechamber, we entered the hall, where Aurelian took his seat, and we – the Doctor, Mikhail and I – stood on the steps down from him, with myself closest to him, the Doctor beside me, and Mikhail and the Lady Clara on the lowest step. Guena was already there. Heralds announced the arrival of Conrad's ambassador, and the Doctor leaned over to whisper in my ear. 'Hope you've got the right guy this time. Be embarrassing to get it wrong again.'

The ambassador was alone, which surprised me, for I had expected at least one servant, if not a whole party, to impress upon us Conrad's strength, and his ability to send whomever he chose across the mountains into our lands. I wondered, watching this man, whether he was the very best that Conrad could send, for he seemed very nervous. Perhaps the weight of the occasion was heavy upon him. 'Your thoughts, Doctor?' I whispered. 'Is this our man?'

'He certainly looks more the part than I do,' he replied. 'Although…'

I was on the alert at once. 'Although what?'

'I was expecting more of an entourage.'

'It's not an easy journey these days,' I said. 'Even with Conrad's aid, our own land can be lawless in places.'

'All the better to bring your guards with you,' he said.

We stopped our whispering then, as Aurelian had risen from his chair to give his formal greetings. 'I am Aurelian,' he said, 'Duke of the Most Ancient, Serene, and Noble State of Varuz. My wife, the Duchess Guena. The Lord Bernhardt. My nephew, the Lord Mikhail. And our guest, the holy man, the Doctor, and his companion, the Lady Clara. We welcome you to our most ancient and noble state, and we wait to hear the messages you bring from your master, Conrad.'

Throughout this speech, the ambassador had been listening politely, but it seemed to me that his attention was not wholly on my lord; indeed, he seemed much distracted by the hall in which we stood, and by his surroundings in general. But when Aurelian had finished, he stepped forwards and gave a pretty speech in turn. 'My lord Duke,' he said. 'The distance between our lands has been too wide in recent years. I hope to get to know your country well. I hope to get to know your city well. And I thank you for your gracious welcome and for the hospitality of your hall. It is,' he said, looking around again, 'a most fine place.'

The Doctor leaned forwards. 'You hope to avoid war?' he said.

'War?' The man sounded horrified. 'I most certainly hope so!'

A few more formalities followed, and then Guena, in her capacity as Duchess and hostess, invited the ambassador to enjoy the hospitality of her home. He looked puzzled at this, and the Doctor interpreted. 'You've had a long journey,' he said. 'She wants to know if you'd like to rest before starting on business.'

'Rest? Rest? Er, yes, that would be very nice, thank you.'

Servants appeared then, and, with courtesy, led

the ambassador away. Aurelian withdrew to his map room, but I lingered to speak to the Doctor privately before joining him. 'Your impressions?' I asked, quietly.

He didn't reply at once. 'I thought...' he said. 'Well, I thought he looked like he was measuring for curtains.'

'I don't understand.'

'He looked like he was trying to work out where his furniture could go, when he and his boss move in.' He must have seen me shivering and nodded ahead. 'Best not say anything to the Duke, eh? Let's keep our eyes set on terms for a peaceful settlement.'

I nodded, and went to join my lord.

There was a feast that evening, to welcome the ambassador, and, while the rations were on the short side, the wine was from old and copious stores, and Clara soon found that she was enjoying herself very much. The Doctor had encouraged her to observe the ambassador, but it was Aurelian that she found herself watching, and admiring. As lord of this hall, and as host to an honoured guest, Aurelian was in his element – convivial, good-tempered, and attentive to his guests. Even Mikhail, sitting a few seats away from his uncle, seemed able to smile when looking at him.

Clara tried to give some attention to her task, engaging the ambassador in small talk, but he was oblique when she quizzed him about his home, and instead wanted to ask questions about the hall, the lights, the décor, the fashions… Only sensible, Clara supposed. He was here on a mission, and if he hadn't visited Varuz before, he would naturally want to know more about the place. Still, she rapidly hit the limits of her knowledge. 'Sorry,' she said. 'I'm new here too.'

Aurelian, however, was more than happy to talk about his ducal possessions, and the ambassador wanted to know about everything. What were the trends in architecture? What were the fashions in clothes? Were precious stones still mined in Varuz, or was what he saw of ancient stock? Did the lights illuminate the whole country? How did the lights work? Did they make new laser-swords? How was this done?

Suddenly, the Duchess spoke, interrupting her husband as he tried his best to answer all these questions. 'My lords,' she said, rising from her chair. The men around the table jumped to their feet; the ambassador slightly behind them, as he realised that to remain sitting would be discourteous. 'It is time for me to retire,' Guena said. She nodded at

Clara. 'Will you accompany me?'

Clara, who, despite the wine, had been paying attention to the way people addressed each other, found an appropriate reply. 'It would be my honour, my lady.'

She followed Guena back to the sitting room where they had had their previous conversation. The room was once again snug and comfortable, and at the ring of the bell, a servant brought in the hot drink they had enjoyed before. With the ambassador now here, Clara was entirely ready to engage in more intrigue, but Guena seemed content to keep their conversation to pleasantries, admiring Clara's dress, or else in providing an interesting if arcane account of the sights one might see in the city, if one had the time. 'Alas,' the Duchess said and sighed. 'Varuz is not what it once was.'

They sat in silence for a while after this statement, as Clara tried to work out what was going on and whether the Duchess was ever going to open up again, and how she might persuade her to do so. Eventually, she took the straightforward route. 'Why am I here?'

'Are you not enjoying our conversation?' said Guena, almost gaily, Clara thought, and with a sly look in her eye. 'I know I certainly am.'

But last time, Clara thought, they hadn't talked about... well, fripperies. Had she imagined the intent of their previous conversation? Had she imagined that the Duchess had wanted her to be a conduit to the ambassador? As the Duchess embarked upon an account of hunting with her father as a child, Clara was starting to feel that way...

A little door at the far end of the chamber opened, and – quietly, unobtrusively – Lord Bernhardt slipped in.

'Oh,' said Clara. 'I see.'

Guena smiled, and turned to her table where, Clara saw now, a third cup had been brought and set ready. As Bernhardt drew up a chair to join them, Guena poured him a drink, which he accepted gratefully. And now, it seemed, Guena was ready to talk business. 'The last time we spoke, Clara,' she said, 'I asked whether you might help us.'

'"Us", is it?' Clara looked at Bernhardt. 'You're in this too?'

'I am the servant of my Duchess,' Bernhardt said quietly. 'If that is what you are asking.'

Clara watched them look at each other. 'Oh,' she said. 'I see. *Us.*'

Guena smiled. Bernhardt did not. In fact, he

looked troubled. As well he might, thought Clara. She wasn't sure what Aurelian would think if he discovered his chief confidant in here with his wife, but she doubted he would be pleased.

'I'm going to be frank with you,' said Clara, 'because I think if we're going to trust each other like this we need to be frank. But doesn't it bother you that you're betraying the Duke? Betraying your country? I mean, I'm not judging – it's up to you and everything – but isn't this a sort of treachery?'

Bernhardt, she saw, had gone very pale. But Guena was looking at her sharply. 'I believe I have mentioned that the last duke was my father.'

Clara considered this significance of this for a moment. 'Oh, I see,' she said, as understanding came. 'Stupid, isn't it? If they'd put you in charge back then, it would probably have saved a whole lot of trouble, wouldn't it?'

Softly, Bernhardt said, 'We are in complete agreement, Clara.' He looked at his Duchess with great love and admiration. 'There is nobody better suited to the rule of his land than my lady. There is nobody who takes the fate of its people more to their heart. I serve the Duke, yes, but my heart is Guena's, and she is the last hope of Varuz.'

'Wow,' breathed Clara at this encomium, and at the look that the two were giving each other, of equal parts great love and trust. 'I hope someone talks like that about me one day. But explain something to me. Mikhail. Why didn't he become Duke?'

Guena sighed. 'He is the son of my younger sister. She, too, is long gone, taken from us much too early, as so many are these days. He was very young when my father died, barely walking. There was a chance of chaos at the death of my father, and this seemed the best arrangement until Mikhail was older.' She looked troubled. 'Perhaps on reflection we might have made better choices.'

'Aurelian's getting a bit above himself, isn't he?' said Clara. 'Inheritance. It's no way to run a government.'

Guena looked at her sternly, but Bernhardt, she saw, was amused.

'Will you help us, Clara?' he said. 'You are someone who can pass unnoticed – but also you are someone who can speak to the ambassador independently. You have seen the straits we are in. Will you approach him on our behalf?'

Clara laughed. 'Approach the representative of a foreign power, who is almost certainly being watched, in order to make overtures of peace that are arguably treasonous? What could possibly go wrong?'

Bernhardt reached for Guena's hand. 'The

secrecy is abominable,' he agreed, seriously. 'It is corrosive. You have my sympathy.'

Clara felt ashamed about joking. These two people were living with this situation every day of their lives, and it was no laughing matter. She felt honoured that they were prepared to trust her. 'I'll speak to him,' she said. 'Of course I will.'

They were both palpably relieved. 'You have our thanks – and, I hope, the thanks of the people of Varuz, if war can be prevented,' said Guena. She turned to the table beside her and reached for a small box. Opening it, she took out a small pendant – a red jewel in an exquisite golden setting. 'Here,' she said and, reaching out, she fastened the pendant around Clara's neck. 'A token of our friendship.'

The light glinted off the facets of the red jewel. 'It's beautiful!'

'It was made a long time ago,' said Guena, 'by a craftsman whose skills are long lost to us. The ancient powers of the royal and noble house are secrets that are now long gone. I wish I could give you something of my own making. But we only have what they left us.'

'I'll look after it,' said Clara. 'Thank you. And I'll do all I can. I don't know what that is – but I'll do all I can.'

Guena and Bernhardt smiled at her, and then at each other. And Bernhardt rested his hand upon his lady's, very lightly, and only for a moment.

Chapter

4

Bernhardt arranged for Clara to have access to the part of the palace where the ambassador had been quartered. 'I can call the guards away quite easily,' he said. 'They will obey me. I will not be able to give you much time without arousing suspicion, however, so slip in, make your case quickly, and leave as soon as you can with whatever answer you get. If the ambassador seems willing to speak, we can arrange another meeting on another day. Speed is essential, and so is secrecy.'

He was as good as his word. When Clara went down to that wing of palace at the agreed hour, she found the way clear. She hurried down the corridor, and tapped lightly on the ambassador's door. He took his time answering, and she found her herself drumming her fingers on the wood, whispering, *Come on… Come on…*

At last he opened the door. 'Lady, um, Clara,' he said in surprise. He looked past her, over her shoulder. 'Are you here alone?'

'Yes.' Clara frowned. 'What's the problem?'

The ambassador pulled the belt on his dressing gown a little tighter. 'I'm not sure that it's… Well, you're a young lady, and I'm not a young… Not in the *least* young when it comes to that… So what I mean is, is this entirely… What I suppose I mean to say is, there's appropriate, and there's, well, *other*, and I'm not sure I know which… Well!'

Clara was tempted to let him flail a while longer, but cruelty wasn't in her nature, and time was of the essence. 'Don't worry,' she said, as she slipped past him into his room, and closed the door behind her. 'You're not my type.' She nearly laughed when she saw his faintly indignant expression. 'Look,' she said, 'we could probably keep going on like this, but I've not got much time. I'm here on behalf of… Well, let's not go into details—'

'That jewel you're wearing,' the ambassador said. 'It's very unusual.'

Clara, knocked slightly off her stride by this unexpected interruption, lifted up the pendant that Guena had given her. 'What, this?'

'Where did you, er… If you don't mind me asking?'

'It was a gift.'

'Oh yes?'

'From the Duchess.'

'Ah,' said the ambassador. 'The Duchess. Very generous of her.'

'They're not really short of material possessions here, you know,' Clara said. 'Not when it comes to this kind of thing. Jewellery, and silver cups, and wall hangings – they're getting a bit frayed, but there are plenty of them. But you can't eat that kind of thing, can you, or mend clothes and wall hangings without new cloth, and so on and so on. They're starting to suffer here. And that's what I'm here about. To find out whether Conrad could lay off at all. Perhaps let a few merchants in over the mountains, or let some boats sail this way, every so often.'

She looked at the ambassador. He was still staring at her necklace.

'Are you listening?'

'Does it have any, er, special properties?' said the ambassador.

'Does it have any *what*?'

'It's hard to explain… Um. How can I explain…?'

'It's a necklace,' said Clara, starting to lose patience. 'Mostly it just hangs around my neck and looks pretty.'

'Mostly?' He was interested in that.

'Figure of speech,' said Clara. 'Mostly as in "entirely".'

'Ah.' The ambassador looked disappointed. 'Never mind. Well, yes, thank you for coming, Lady, er, yes… Yes, thank you for coming…'

'We've not talked yet!' Clara exclaimed, but the ambassador was already manoeuvring her back towards the door. 'I've got a whole speech to give you yet! There are people who want to reach out to you!'

'No need, no need for any more… Yes, I understand. The usual business. People here want change. Asked you to ask me to speak to the, er… yes, Conrad… asked you to ask me to speak to Conrad on their behalf. And of course I will – absolutely I will! What else am I here for?' He opened the door and all but shoved Clara out into the corridor. 'No, no!' he said loudly, for the benefit of anyone passing. 'You want the *next* corridor, I believe! Yes, the next one!'

And the door was shut firmly in Clara's face. 'All right then,' she said to the door. 'I suppose that's the job done.' She looked quickly around her, but the corridor was clear, so she took advantage of her opportunity, and slipped back to her own rooms, where the Doctor was waiting.

'And?' he said, when she came in.

'And he's an odd one,' Clara said. 'Didn't let me stay longer than a few minutes. I know I only intended to *stay* for a few minutes, but I'd rather it had been on my terms.'

'It's quite understandable,' said the Doctor. 'He'd be concerned for his mission if he was found talking behind Aurelian's back. It might get him chucked out. So what did you say to him? What did he have to say?'

'Not much on either side,' Clara admitted. 'Mostly what he wanted to talk about was this.' She held up her pendant and the Doctor, seeming to notice it for the first time, ran his sonic screwdriver over the jewel, frowning as he did so. 'It was like he was expecting it to shoot death rays at him. I'm not saying I'd turn down a necklace like that – that would be a real fashion statement, wouldn't it? – but...' She laughed. 'Not very likely, is it?'

The Doctor was staring down at his sonic. 'No?'

Clara touched the pendant carefully. 'It won't, will it?'

'What, shoot death rays?' He shook his head. 'I shouldn't think so.'

'Good!'

The Doctor twisted the sonic round in his hand. 'Although it might give you the odd electric shock.'

'What!' Clara grabbed the jewel and held it in the palm of her hand, looking at it suspiciously.

He tapped the sonic. 'There's some kind of energy emitting from it. Haven't a clue what. Probably innocuous.'

'*Probably* innocuous?' Clara started to unclasp the thing. 'That's the kind of phrase which pops up in obituaries. "The rays, which had been thought probably innocuous, turned out to be flipping lethal."'

'I'll write you a better obituary than that, Clara, I promise. Hey!' He reached out his hand. 'Don't take it off!'

'I'm not wearing this! Energy emissions! Death rays!'

'Death rays unproven,' he said. 'Besides, if the Duchess sees you're not wearing it, she'll be offended.'

'If it's so innocuous, you can wear it!'

The Doctor shook his head. 'Oh, no. I'm not really one for—'

'Yes,' said Clara, 'I know. Fripperies.' She ran her finger along the jewel's golden setting. Suddenly the pendant felt very heavy.

'It's safe, Clara,' the Doctor said. 'I promise. But we've learned one thing – the ambassador is as interested in the technology of Varuz as I am. I wonder why. You know, there's a lot that doesn't add up there…' He frowned. 'You noticed earlier that Guena stopped Aurelian before he talked too much about the objects around the palace.'

'Yes, I noticed that.' Clara frowned. 'What? Do you think Guena is double-crossing us?'

'No,' said the Doctor. 'I believe she wants peace – or, rather, that she doesn't want war. But I don't think she's told us everything. The Duchess has a great deal more up her sleeve, I'm sure of that. Perhaps that's part of what the ambassador has been sent to find out – exactly what's left over here from their glory days. What the people of Varuz have tucked up their sleeves beyond electric light and fancy swords.'

And necklaces that came with built-in death rays. Clara went to bed (the necklace lay on a table beside her) thinking over what the Doctor had said. She slept well, despite their discussion, which was fortunate, as it was the last night's sleep she was to have in a comfortable bed for quite some time. The next morning, she and the Doctor were woken early by a hammering on the door to their chambers. The palace guard was there, summoning them to come before the Duke – and they didn't look very friendly.

*

75

I came to the Great Hall as quickly as I could, running through the palace, but slowing to a walk before entering the hall itself. Nothing would be served by allowing the court to see the Duke's chief adviser in a state of panic. When I reached the hall I beheld a sight that I had long dreaded that I might witness: Lord Mikhail, between armed guards, standing before my lord. I saw the Doctor too, off to one side, with Lady Clara beside him. He gestured to me to join them, and I slipped quietly around the hall, my eyes on Mikhail all the while. *'Use your sense, lad,'* I murmured to myself. *'Use those wits you have inherited from your grandsire. And do not lie to him. He will know – and it will only make him angry…'* So thinking, I reached the Doctor.

But Mikhail, it seemed, still believed that he could conceal whatever plans he had made. 'This is a dreadful accusation, sir, and I deny it. Have I not served you loyally? Have I not obeyed you in all things, as a child growing up within your court, and now, as a man, as one of your knights? My Lord Duke, how could you believe me capable of a treachery such as this?'

'Hold your tongue, lad,' I muttered, for I could see upon his face, and in his closing fists, the signals that my lord Duke was about to lose his temper.

'Do you think I am a fool?' Aurelian said. 'You

were *seen*! People saw you in that part of the palace!'

Mikhail drew a breath. 'Then it seems that they misunderstood, sir,' he said and, for a moment, I wondered whether he was telling the truth. His strategy was, otherwise, going to be ruinous, should Aurelian have proof of his disloyalty. 'Yes, I was in that part of that palace, but no meeting happened—'

'Liar!' Aurelian said. 'You were seen leaving his *rooms*!'

Ah, so he was caught then, the young lord. Poor lad; his face went deathly white. My instinct, as ever, was to protect him – but before I could step forwards to speak my piece, the Doctor, who must have seen me move, put his hand upon my arm to restrain me. 'Wait,' he murmured. 'Mikhail has made his decision, and must be allowed to take his own course. It's long past time he was allowed to be his own man.'

And indeed the young lord was gathering himself together, and I could see that he was no longer cowed. To Aurelian, he said, 'You have been spying on me.'

'With justification,' said the Duke.

'A dishonourable act, sir.'

'To deal with a dishonourable man.' Aurelian shook his head. 'After all that I have done for you!'

Mikhail's eyes blazed. Now, truly, I saw his ancestry. How much he looked like his grandsire then! *'Done* for me? How dare you! You dispossessed me! You took my seat – this seat, the ancient dukedom of Varuz! You took it for your own, and then you blamed me for mistrusting you! Ever since I was a boy, you have watched me as if I was a viper in the nest—'

'With reason, boy!' Aurelian snapped back. 'I knew you would prove faithless – and so it has turned out.'

'You're a fool, sir,' Mikhail said, coldly. 'And if it were only your own ruin you were causing, I would not care. But you have brought Varuz to the brink of destruction, and you do not listen when your knights try to tell you that your strategies are madness! I have nothing to lose, for you have stolen it all from me, so I *will* have my say now! We cannot defeat Conrad in open war! But even at this late hour we can still make a peace that will let something of Varuz survive—'

Suddenly, Aurelian drew his sword. The light that was contained within blazed forth. 'Mikhail,' he said. 'I strip you of your titles. I strip you of your rank. And I banish you henceforth from all lands under my rule. Leave Varuz.'

There were gasps from around the hall. Clara,

watching the young man blanch, stepped forwards and said, 'You can't do that! That's not fair! He's trying to stop you from getting everyone killed!'

But Aurelian had barely begun his day's work. He turned on Clara. 'I know you're in league,' he said. 'You, him, and the other one.' He pointed towards the ambassador, who was standing by the wall, trying to make himself invisible. Yes, I recognise that strategy when I see it, for I have used it often myself. 'Conrad's vassal,' Aurelian said. 'Do you think I'm a fool? Do you think I am not lord of this hall? Your meetings have not gone unnoticed.' He turned to the ambassador. 'There isn't a dungeon deep enough in which to imprison you.' He looked back at Clara. 'Nor you, lady.'

'Er, Doctor,' muttered Clara, 'I'm not liking the sound of this…'

Aurelian, eyes flashing, turned upon the Doctor. 'Yes, and you – I trusted you, above all! Did you know about all this?'

The Doctor was looking at him with unveiled contempt. 'Oh, for the love of… Will you sit down, man! Don't be such a fool!'

'A *fool*!'

I thought that things were about to take a very evil turn, but then the Duchess rose from her seat. Now I knew I must step forwards, and even as I did so, I felt the Doctor's hand upon my arm, trying to restrain me. 'Guena!' I cried out. 'No—!' But too late.

'Enough,' she said. 'This must stop.' She turned to her husband. 'Aurelian, if you banish these people, you must banish me. For I am the architect of this conspiracy.'

It felt to Clara as if the Duchess of Varuz had suddenly revealed all her power. Yes, she had known that Guena was intelligent, and shrewd, and that the woman commanded great respect from the people around her but, watching her now, Clara thought that so far she had been allowed to see only a little of Guena's strength. Her admiration for the Duchess only increased when Guena spoke. She could have left them all to cover for her, Clara thought – and they would have done. She, and Bernhardt, and Mikhail – they would not have revealed who had asked them to approach the ambassador. But she had not let them take the fall.

'Yes, Aurelian,' she said. 'The young woman, Clara, went to speak to the ambassador at my request. If you are to imprison anyone, sir, then you must imprison me.'

Aurelian stared at her, utterly wrong-footed.

His anger had completely dissipated and now he looked devastated. Clara had to feel sorry for him. '*Guena?*' he said. 'What do you mean?'

The Duchess rested one hand, heavy with rings, upon his arm. 'Aurelian,' she said. 'Listen to me, now. There has been no battle, but already we are all but defeated. We are all but lost. You want to take us to war – but if there is war, that will be the end. There will be no more Varuz. If you bring war to Conrad, he will not hold back. He will make an example of us that will never be forgotten upon this green world.' She looked at the ambassador, cowering against the wall. 'If you kill this man, if you harm him or even, I think, if you shame him – you will bring that anger down upon us. You will bring about our end. Send him home, if you must, but let him go unmolested. And, sir,' she said, lifting her voice and addressing the ambassador directly, 'tell your master that the Duchess of Varuz remembers herself to him, and that she asks him to remember her, and believe her when she says that she hopes that they will meet again upon this green world in happier days, as friends, and not as enemies.'

Aurelian was standing in thought, head bowed. He turned to the ambassador and, in quieter tones, said, 'Leave. Go back to your master. Take my lady's message to him. And… take the girl.'

At a nod from Aurelian, guards began to move towards Clara. 'Doctor,' she said, uneasily, 'what's going on? "The girl"? Does he mean me? Go where?'

The Doctor, however, she could see, was thinking – quickly, and hard. He put his hand upon Clara's shoulder, and pushed her towards the ambassador. 'Go with him,' he said. 'Go with him now.'

'What?'

'War's coming, Clara, whatever the Duchess thinks her message might do. But you'll be safe with the ambassador.'

'I don't want to be safe!'

'Don't underestimate it—'

'Doctor!'

'Clara…' He leaned in, grasping her arm, firmly but kindly, and he spoke very quietly. 'Listen to me. Yes, I want you to be safe. Don't blame me for that. But there's something else. You've got a job to do now – don't you see? An important job, perhaps the most important one there is right now. Go with the ambassador. Go with him to *Conrad*…'

'Oh,' Clara breathed. 'Yes, I see.'

'Yes, yes, I knew you would!' The Doctor smiled, and pressed her shoulder. 'Get yourself to Conrad. Explain that you're not from Varuz, that you're a visitor, but in the time you've been here you've got to know the place and its people, and you know they want peace. And,' he nodded towards the ambassador, 'stick with him. There's something else going on there and I want to know what. Find out for me.'

The guards were drawing closer, hands upon the hilts of their swords.

'Is that enough to be getting on with, Clara? Unsafe enough for you?'

'Doctor,' she said, 'how do I contact you? I could end up miles away—'

'Don't worry!' he said. 'We'll find a way!'

The nearest of the guards gestured to Clara that she should follow. 'All right! All right!' she said. 'I'm coming!'

The Doctor gave her one last encouraging squeeze on the arm, and then she and the ambassador were led away. As she left the hall, she looked back over her shoulder, to see Aurelian turn to Bernhardt.

'And you, sir,' Aurelian said. 'I believe you are more caught up in this than I would like.' Suddenly, Aurelian looked crushed, and old. 'Bernhardt,' he said, 'you too? My old friend. My brother. How could you?'

*

I realised, as I stood before Aurelian, that I had always expected it to come to this. I had long feared that my duplicity would at some point be brought into the open, and that I would be called upon to account for my betrayal. For myself, I cared little, and my chief concern now was to protect the honour of my lady. If I was to be thrown to the wolves, Guena was not to be ruined with me. Varuz would need her fearlessness when the end came. I, meanwhile, was dispensable. So, yes, I had imagined this scene many times in the dark watches of the night; I had prepared myself, and I had believed, after such long practice, that I could face it with equanimity. What I had not prepared myself for was what would happen next. How could I? None of us could have guessed what was to happen next, not even the Doctor.

To understand why the next events had such great impact, you must understand the extent to which we were in disarray. News had passed swiftly around the city of Mikhail's exposure, of the ambassador's shaming, of Lady Clara's banishment. Those lords and knights who had not already been at the palace had hurried to see what turn these events would take next. Almost the whole court was there to see me stand before Aurelian and try to justify myself to him.

'Lord,' I said, and opened out my hands in supplication. 'I will deny nothing. The Duchess came to me, it is true, to ask for advice – but she found me a keen listener, and one who urged her forward in her attempts to contact the ambassador and try for peace.' Behind me, I could hear the assembled court, holding its collective breath, waiting to see what Aurelian would do in the face of this frank confession. 'I will not lie to you, Aurelian,' I said, and I saw him flinch at the use of his name. 'We are falling apart. We must do something, or else this city and its people will be gone before the end of this year. I could not see that anything was being done. So I took it upon myself to act—'

'You took it upon yourself,' Aurelian said, very quietly, and for one brief second I feared for my life. Behind me, too, I heard the court murmur and whisper, as if certain that the order for my execution was close at hand.

And then everything changed.

No herald announced their arrival. No silver trumpets sounded to accompany their way through the streets to our palace. No sign had been given or message conveyed to the Duke to say that they approached. No, it was as if they were not there – and then they were there.

A company of thirty knights, and their captain. Grave knights, and grim, heavily armoured, their tabards richly coloured with strange devices. Their faces were hidden behind the great masks of their helmets, the flesh of their hands was hidden behind great gloves. For the merest moment, I did not believe that anything alive inhabited those suits of armour – and then the knights moved, and marched through the hall.

They came forwards in complete silence other than the pounding of their boots, and that silence spread. All our quarrels ceased. Reaching Aurelian, they came to a halt, lining up, five rows of six, and their captain towards the front. He wore the same armour and the same devices as the others, but his helmet bore a red crest.

Beside me, I heard the Doctor muttering to himself. I saw him slip his hand into his pocket, and he drew forth a short, thin piece of metal, as long as a dagger, perhaps, but not sharpened to a blade. This he cupped to hide within his hand. I heard a low humming sound, like bees might make on a summer's day, and the Doctor continued talking to himself. '*Mechanical?*' he said. '*Not mechanical? No, no, hard to tell… What are they?*'

Their captain stepped forward. I saw the palace guards move to protect their Duke, but Aurelian halted them with one quick movement of his hand. 'Sir,' he said, 'you bring a strange company into our midst. Who are you, sir?'

The captain of the company removed his helmet.

That face…

Never have I seen the like in all my long years upon this green world. Great beauty, mixed with great age, and, above all, an almost overwhelming weariness.

'Good lord of this hall,' he said, with courtesy. 'And the brave knights gathered here. My name is Lancelot. I come here from a city named Ravenna.'

'Sir,' said Aurelian. 'You and your company are welcome to my hall.' He looked upon the knight in wonder. 'But what brings you here? What is your mission amongst us?'

'Sir,' said Lancelot, 'In the name of Arthur the King, the Duke of Britain, I seek the Holy Grail.'

I saw the Doctor's face, and I heard his muttered oath, and I knew that he was utterly taken by surprise. And that – more than the fear of exposure, more than the presence of these grim and terrible knights – that above all was what made me afraid.

Chapter

5

In the days that followed, I found myself travelling with this captain, Lord Lancelot, and his company of knights on a journey that took us into the wild. When men travel together, and particularly in a time of war, they learn much about each other: they learn what makes others laugh and weep; they learn the farthest reaches of their courage; they see the very worst and the very best of each other. But I learned little of Lancelot and his men beyond what I saw then. They did not laugh. They did not weep. They sought the Grail, whatever that might be, and, when it came to that quest, their tenacity was boundless. Beyond that, however, there was nothing. They might have been empty suits of armour for all that they felt the sorrow of life, aye, and its joy.

For now, however, they were a mystery, even

to the one amongst us who seemed to know something of them. 'Who is this knight, Doctor?' I whispered. 'Do you know him?'

'Know him?' he hissed back. 'How can I know him? Lancelot and the Grail are a story!'

'They appear in no story that I know, Doctor,' I said, with confidence, for although I was no scholar, I was as learned as a man can be in such a time, when the trials and perils of border war leave little time for study or reflection.

'Not from here,' he said. 'They're from Clara's world – but the point is that they didn't exist. Yes, parts of that story were true, but not Lancelot of the Lake and the Grail Quest. They were invented centuries later. In fact, the last time I met anyone claiming to be the Knights of King Arthur they turned out to be from another dimension.'

'And Ravenna?'

'A city. Quite a beautiful one too. A capital, at one point.'

'On Clara's world,' I said, for I had not failed to notice this, and I had marked too that he had not claimed Clara's world as his own.

He gave me a steady look. 'That's right,' he said, offering no more.

We studied each other for a moment or two, and then I turned the matter aside, for there was enough to consider beyond what this might imply. 'Invention or not these knights are assuredly here now,' I said.

'I can see that!' the Doctor snapped. 'I bet they're conmen,' he muttered. 'Yes, that'll be it. There are a lot of conmen out there, trying to pinch people's Crown Jewels.'

I looked at Aurelian. A light seemed to be shining from him as he stood before Lancelot. 'My lord Duke is much impressed.'

And indeed it was hard to think of a welcome as lavish as the one Aurelian gave to this company then. I wonder if perhaps this, in part, is what caused the Doctor's dismay. Barely two days had passed since Aurelian had been greeting him with smiles and full honour. And now he was forgotten. Yet I could see why Aurelian's affections had transferred. For while the Doctor was compelling – and indeed he remained so to me, as strong and fierce as metal – yet against these knights something of his allure was diminished. His austerity and directness were nothing beside their mystery and glamour, and these were qualities that appealed to Aurelian. For myself, I would always take the strength of steel above the glitter of gold.

'Come now,' said Aurelian to Lancelot. 'Sit upon my chair. Tell me about your journeys, and this

Grail which you seek.'

'Go on,' said the Doctor. 'Tell him all about it. I dare you.'

Lancelot turned his head to look at the Doctor, barely registering his presence before turning away again to Aurelian. 'It is a long story, and much of it is lost in the mists of time.'

Again, Aurelian gestured to his seat. 'Sit, sir,' he said. 'I would hear all about it.'

And Lancelot sat, slowly, as if his old bones had forgotten how to be at rest, and he remained upright in the seat, as if he might depart at a moment's notice, should his quest demand. Resting his gloved hands upon his knees, he opened his mouth to speak.

'Oh,' muttered the Doctor, 'this should be worth hearing.'

And indeed we heard a great tale then, a tale of marvels, of the man who had been king and would be king once again; of that king's battles against his invaders; of his fair court and his circle of knights, and their great quest. And there they were, this company, and they stood silent and helmeted throughout all this long tale.

'And here we are,' said Lancelot, at last. 'Here we are. We seek the greatest treasure, lord. We seek the Holy Grail.'

Aurelian was looking at him with great wonder and love upon his face. 'I have never heard these tales before. How could that be? What strange world fashioned you, wanderer? Where could you come from?'

'Yes,' said the Doctor. 'I think I'd like to know that too.'

'I have come,' said Lancelot, 'from a land beyond the black of night. I have come from a land more distant than all the stars that you can see in your heavens.'

Aurelian gave a deep sigh of loss and longing. 'A land beyond the stars,' he said. 'They say our forefathers, at their high point, walked amongst the stars.'

Guena, sitting beside Lancelot, started. 'They say many things about our forefathers, my lord. Only some are true. Many are fantasies – or desires.'

'And much has been concealed,' said Aurelian, sharply, before turning back to Lancelot. 'But this Grail,' he said. 'I have not heard enough about this. Tell me about it.'

'An object of great beauty and power,' Lancelot replied. 'The vessel which contained the blood of the redeemer. A symbol of perfection and of life beyond death.'

'Yes, yes…!' Aurelian was rapt. 'Such a symbol

would be a great gift to the finder…'

The Doctor stepped forwards. 'Except this is all made up, isn't it?' Even to me, who was his greatest ally in this court, his voice sounded harsh and unwelcome. 'None of it's true. Oh yes, there was a King Arthur,' he said, 'or someone close enough. King would be pushing it. He was a warlord, in a time of failure and collapse.' He looked pointedly at Aurelian. 'They called him a Duke, too. He was someone who took the job because there was no one else left to do it. But there wasn't a Grail. There wasn't a Lancelot. All that was made up. No, it's worse than that. It was all made up by the *French*.'

'Doctor,' I said, softly.

He span round to look at me. 'What?'

'Look to the court,' I said, for there was much anger and muttering at this speech. 'This does not help your cause.'

'Then it should,' he said. 'This is the help you need. All of this,' he gestured round, taking in Lancelot and the company, 'isn't what it seems. There is something else going on, I'll bet you every single jewel in this palace.' He turned to Lancelot. 'So what's the con? You can't really believe the Grail is here?'

'This is where the quest has brought us,' Lancelot replied, and I was struck at how uncaring he was at the Doctor's assault upon him. It was not that he was being patient, or attempting to curry his favour. He simply did not care.

'How?' said the Doctor. 'What's made you believe that? Was there a story? A map? Did you talk to a Sphinx or an Oracle? Or did you pull the idea out of your own addled brains, because I am telling you – you will not find the Holy Grail here. You'll not find it anywhere. Because it doesn't exist.'

Aurelian stepped forwards. 'Be silent, Doctor! Your part in the conspiracy against me is not yet clear.' Turning to Lancelot, he said, 'I believe you, sir. You are clearly a knight of great lineage and honour. And I am the Duke here. I command.' Then he turned to face the hall, addressed his own knights, filling the space with his loud clear voice. 'Hear me now, noble lords of Varuz. At the very moment of our defeat, we have been offered a second chance. This Grail is an object of great power. It could be our salvation. Therefore I ask you now, who amongst you loves his lord and his land enough to seek this Grail? Who will join this company on their quest?'

If I have given thus far the impression of weakness on Aurelian's part, this is only because I have been speaking of his latter days. There was a reason we had chosen him for the Dukedom, however. At the height of his powers he had the gift of rallying people, of bringing them to him, of giving them heart.

Alas, those days were long gone for Aurelian. Now a dreadful silence met his call to action. All of us, his knights, I saw, were looking elsewhere, at anything or anyone but him.

'What?' he cried. 'Is there nobody here who will meet this challenge?'

And it seemed that there was not. We were at odds with one another, unless something could be found to unite us…

The guards allowed Clara to detour briefly past her rooms to change from her gown into something more suitable for travelling, and to pack some items for the journey. Then she was hurried to the palace gates. The ambassador was already there, with the same grey-haired knight, who, with Lord Mikhail, had taken Clara and the Doctor to the palace on their first day. When Clara arrived, the knight addressed her and the ambassador in formal terms.

'By the order of Aurelian, Duke of the Most Ancient, Serene, and Noble State of Varuz, you are required to leave the lands beneath his rule by sunrise, under penalty of death—'

'All right, all right,' said Clara, 'we've got the idea. And banishing us is all very well, and I've every intention of doing what I'm told, but I'm a stranger to these parts. Which way do we go? And how do we get past Conrad's men? Aren't they guarding all the routes out?'

The knight took pity on her. 'The road runs along the river, and will take you to the foothills of the mountains. When the river bends away from the road, follow its course. You will find the mountain path. This is the quickest way to the border. As for Conrad's men...' He shook his head. 'There I cannot help you, and you must throw yourself upon the mercy of your travelling companion, should he travel the whole way with you. And to both of you, I would say – beware of bandits in the mountains. This land is not as lawful as it was.'

'Bandits,' said Clara. 'Great. Any chance we could borrow one of those laser-swords? No,' she said, when the man smiled and shook his head. 'I didn't think there was.'

And then it was time to go. The guards led them through the city gates, and watched them as they went on their way. The journey was smooth at first, the road so near the city being in relatively good repair, although as the morning went on, more cracks appeared in the great flat upper stones, revealing the gravel beneath. In places, the road was no better than a muddy path.

The ambassador proved not much of a conversationalist, which made the walk rather dreary. Still, Clara didn't blame him; he must not be looking forward to returning home to report the complete failure of his mission. He seemed to want to delay their journey too: stopping all of a sudden to stray off the path to examine some old building as they passed – an abandoned cottage, or a tumbledown wall, or some other piece of broken stone that grabbed his attention.

As the day wore on, civilisation, such it was, fell completely away from them. The river ran on beside them, rushing back towards the city, and ahead the mountains began to loom large. At last they reached the place where the road and the river diverged. The road swung northwards, while the river carried on east into the mountains. On the southern bank, Clara could see the remains of another old road, heading south, but the bridge was in ruins, and there was no easy way to cross. The river was deep, and wide, and fast-flowing.

'All right,' Clara said. 'What was the route you used to come in?'

'Hmm?' said the ambassador.

'You got through to Varuz somehow. How did

you get here?'

'Well, you know…' The ambassador gestured vaguely ahead. 'Through the, um, through the those…'

'The those?'

'The, um, the mountains.'

Clara looked at the peaks rising up ahead. 'There are quite a lot of mountains,' she said, and sighed. 'Look, I know you don't want to give away state secrets, such as the sneaky route out of Varuz, but I'm going to have to come with you—'

'Oh no!' said the ambassador in horror. 'No, I don't think so! Oh no, that's simply not possible at all!'

Clara tried to stay patient. 'I don't want to tell you your business, but we've got a major diplomatic incident on our hands. You've just been sent away from Aurelian's court! I'm assuming Conrad isn't going to take that lightly. It could be exactly the excuse he needs to invade.'

'I don't understand why that means you want to come with me!' He looked around wildly. 'Can't you… I don't know… find a quiet spot here? Yes, it really is lovely here, nice and remote, well away from everything. You could sit here until whatever trouble is coming has passed—'

'I could,' said Clara, 'but I'm not going to. Don't

you understand that I'm on your side? Well,' she corrected herself, 'I'm not on anyone's side, but I don't want a war and I hope you don't want to see one either.'

The ambassador nodded fervently.

'There you are,' said Clara. 'The Duchess asked me to speak to you on her behalf, and through you to send a message to Conrad. So why don't I speak to Conrad directly? If I can meet him, talk to him – I can tell him that the Duchess and others want peace. He'll see that even if the Duke has sent you away, there are many people in Varuz who want to talk and find a way out of this impasse.'

The ambassador was staring down at his hands. 'Hmm, well, let me think about it.'

'What is there to think about?'

He squirmed. 'There are complications…'

'What complications?' Clara said. 'Tell me about them. I'm a great listener and I'm full of bright ideas. I might be able to help you uncomplicate your complications.'

'Oh, no, I couldn't do that!'

'Why not?' said Clara.

The ambassador drew himself up grandly. 'State business.'

Clara sighed. 'Oh, all right,' she said. 'But I'm still coming with you. I can't stay here, can I? I've been banished. If I hang around here, chances are someone will come after me with a laser-sword. You too.'

That was enough to get them moving again. They walked on upwards for a long time, both deep in thought, as the day declined and the darkness began to settle around them. When they reached a small stream splashing down from the heights, Clara suggested they stop and rest for the night. The ambassador readily agreed, so they found a spot beneath the trees, and began to make camp.

'How far are we from the border?' Clara asked.

'Not far, I think. Still a good walk. Uphill, you know.'

Clara peered into the shadows, looking for the faintest glimmer of a laser-sword. 'Well, I know they said sunrise to get off their land, but we've done our best and we've come a long way. Surely they won't mind if we spend one last night here in Varuz. At least we're heading in the right direction.'

They made themselves as comfortable as possible – Clara thought sadly of the great soft bed back in the palace – but the day had been very long, and she quickly fell fast asleep.

Only to wake, suddenly, in the dead of night. She sat up, and peered around, looking for the ambassador, but there was no sign of him. Nor, she realised as she squinted into the darkness, was there any sign of his possessions – they were gone, as if someone had packed up and left. With a sudden insight, and rising sense of dread, she checked around her neck for Guena's pendant that Guena had given her. Gone.

Clara jumped up. The ambassador could have taken one of only two routes. Either he was heading back down the mountain to the river, or else he was going on ahead. Clara hesitated. Perhaps he had a river route home. She had no way of knowing. All she knew for sure was that back might involve lasers, while ahead would eventually lead to Conrad. She packed hurriedly, and ran on up the mountain.

As it turned out, the ambassador hadn't got very far. Taking the pendant must have been what had disturbed her sleep, and he was blundering uphill with a woeful lack of stealth. Soft-footedly, Clara slid up behind him, and tapped him on the shoulder. It nearly sent him into orbit. He swung round and stared at her in fright.

'All right, sunshine,' she said, as she might when speaking to a particularly irritating Year Seven specimen. 'What's going on? Where are you heading? And why have you nicked my necklace?'

For a moment, she thought the ambassador was

going to make an undignified run for it. Then he pressed his hands against his chest. 'Oh, my poor heart.'

'Lay off the drama,' she said firmly. The teacher voice was working well on this one. 'Tell me what you're up to and where you're going.'

'It's difficult to explain,' he said. 'You won't believe me.'

The first, faintest glimmer of dawn was starting to break through. 'Try me,' said Clara. 'I can believe several impossible things before breakfast.'

The hall remained silent. Aurelian's call to action hung in the air, but nobody answered.

'What?' my lord cried. 'Is there not one of you who will meet this challenge? Where are the knights of Varuz? Have they abandoned their home, their hall, their Duke? '

How my heart went out to Aurelian. Here he stood, in front of his noble guest and those grim men, trying to rally his own knights, but not a single one stepped forwards at his request. He had not deserved this, I thought; for throughout his life, first as knight and then as Duke, he had tried to serve the land and its people. I saw tears in his eyes, but he spoke strongly still.

'Shame on you!' he cried, into the silence. 'Are

you nobles of Varuz? Where is your heart? Your strength? Your pride?'

I looked away. My own heart was filled with that shame, because I knew that their loss of faith in Aurelian was in no small part my fault. When I dared to look up at the other nobles, I could see the doubt in their eyes. The arrival of Lancelot had not made them completely forget the scene that had been unfolding beforehand. They knew that Aurelian stood alone. His wife no longer trusted him. And I – they knew – I too had shown that I no longer had faith in him…

'Nobody?' said Aurelian.

'Nobody,' muttered the Doctor. 'And good for them. This should put a stop to this whole business…'

I could not bear this any longer. This was not what Aurelian deserved. Stepping forwards, I walked towards him. I saw the palace guard make a move, but I still carried enough sway that they would not touch me willingly, and I reached Aurelian unmolested. We stood face-to-face and eye-to-eye.

'My lord,' I said, quietly. 'I know that you doubt me – and I cannot blame you. I have looked to speak to the representative of our enemy behind your back. I have sought to undermine your policies. But you and I...' I held out my hands, hoping to make him recall our friendship. 'We have been closer than brothers. Time and again, we have fought together under the red banner. For years, we walked together along the border passes, denying our enemy, protecting our people. You and I – we both love this land.'

Aurelian looked away from me. 'And yet only one of us has remained true.'

'I hope that one day you will understand,' I said. 'I *am* loyal, my lord – to Varuz. Above all I wish to see her people safe.'

Aurelian gave me an angry look. 'And you say that I do not?'

I was conscious as we were speaking of three things. First, that there was a hushed silence, and my companions-in-arms were listening closely to this exchange. Second, I was aware of the intense scrutiny with which the Doctor was watching me. And last of all, and most strange, I could not help but be alert to the utter impassivity of Lancelot and his company as this scene unfolded before them. They were silent, incurious – almost as if they had absented themselves from the room whilst this exchange happened. They cared nothing for our heartache and our sorrows, for our sense of grief at our division and the strife between us. It meant nothing to them.

'My lord,' I said. 'Of course you are true too – how could anyone doubt that? It is only that we disagree on what is best for Varuz—'

'And so now you wish to lecture me, yes?' he said bitterly. 'You wish to tell me that this is a foolish quest, that I should give up on Varuz and hand her to Conrad? You are a wise man, Bernhardt, but sometimes wisdom leads you to passivity. You think yourself out of action.'

'You misunderstand me, my lord.' Slowly, formally, I knelt down before him. 'Aurelian – you have asked whether there is one of your knights willing to ride with this company. And there is one. I will ride with them, if that is what you desire. I will take up their quest for this Grail, whatever that might be, if you require it. If you believe that this is how I can best serve Varuz.'

Guena, I saw, was shaking her head. But Aurelian said, 'Yes. Yes, that is what I require.'

And so I lifted my voice so that all present could hear. 'Knights of Varuz,' I cried, 'all of you gathered here – join me now. The Duke requires our loyalty and our unity. So let us show him how we share a common purpose – the love of our lord and our great land. Let us be the knights that we were born to be!'

Aurelian offered me his hands and, taking them, I let him lift me again to my feet. The court was now abuzz. The Doctor came across to me. 'Bernhardt. You know better than this.'

'I only know what my duty is, Doctor.'

'But this is a waste of time! There's no such thing as the Grail—'

'What does that matter?' I said back. 'Look! Look at the men of the court! They are gathering together at last.'

And it was true. The knights of Varuz, who had been lost, were now taking behind the cause. I turned to Aurelian, and saw what I had longed to see – a glimmer of hope in his eyes where, for years now, there had only been growing despair. I thought, *If we can bring some hope to Aurelian, perhaps we can still bring some hope to Varuz…*

'That's all very well,' said the Doctor, 'But is anyone going to tell Aurelian how this story ends? Hey, Lancelot? Are you going to tell him or shall I?'

Now Lancelot spoke to him. Turning to the Doctor, he said, 'The story has not ended. The quest goes on – and now it is strengthened with new blood.'

Chapter

6

Sitting on the hillside, with the dawn light steadily strengthening around them, Clara listened as the ambassador began his explanation. 'First,' he said, 'I'm going to have to ask you to accept something marvellous and extraordinary.'

'Go on,' said Clara.

'I know you're a traveller, Clara, but I'm going to ask to you imagine that there are lands beyond the ones you know. Lands that are so distant, you could not travel there in your lifetime, even with the fastest vessel you could imagine.'

Clara smiled. 'Are you talking about space flight?'

The ambassador stared at her. 'What?'

'You *are* talking about space flight, aren't you?' She laughed. 'You know, you can skip that bit. You really can.'

'You know something about space travel?'

'Oh yes. Chances are I know slightly more about that you do,' said Clara, and decided not to mention the bit about travelling through time. That might well make things too complicated for now. 'So you're not from around these parts, eh? Join the club.'

The ambassador's eyes widened in shock. 'You're not from this world either?'

'Funny old business, life, isn't it?' Clara said. 'Throws up all sorts of odd coincidences. Who would have thought? Big universe, small world. Yes, I'm an alien too. Just passing, and got all mixed up in something. As usual.'

The ambassador scratched his cheek. 'This has never happened to me before. A lifetime of travelling, and this has never happened to me before.'

'No?' said Clara. 'You need to get out more. Or visit a better class of planet. The universe is *teeming* with life. So, go on, what's the deal? Why are you here? It's a bit off the beaten track, isn't it?'

'It's true that this world is something of a galactic backwater. But then I suppose that my interests are quite specialist.'

'Specialist?' Clara frowned. 'That sounds like it could be dodgy.'

'I am interested,' said the ambassador grandly,

'in strange and beautiful things.'

'Well, who isn't?' said Clara. 'But what do you mean, "interested"? Are you an art dealer? A treasure hunter? An archaeologist? You know, you don't look very much like Indiana Jones.'

Now the ambassador was completely bewildered. 'Indiana who?'

'Forget it,' said Clara. 'It'll only complicate things further. What kind of things are you interested in, and why?'

The ambassador gladly took refuge in the safety of this question. 'I'm a collector,' he said, proudly.

'A collector? What do you collect? Stamps? Vinyl? Teapots?'

'Sometimes, some of those. But mostly I collect interesting devices. Technology and gadgetry from all across the galaxy.'

'You should come to Earth,' said Clara.

'Oh, is *that* where you're from?' The ambassador smiled. 'That was a very interesting world. Full of trinkets—'

'Don't say digital watches,' muttered Clara.

'Well, yes, obviously, but not only. I'm interested in how things work, you see. I'm interested in the things that people build and why they make them. It's usually to make life easier in some way – but not always.'

'So what did you want with my pendant?' Seeing the ambassador's guilty expression, she went on, fiercely: 'No, I haven't forgotten, and I'll have it back, thank you very much.'

Sheepishly, he dug into his pocket and handed it over.

Clara put it back around her neck. Death rays or not, it was hers, and she was keeping it. 'What did you want this for?' she said. 'It's not a gadget – it's decorative. Ornamentation. Almost what you might call a frippery. So what do you want with a necklace, assuming you really aren't just a jewel thief?'

'I am most certainly not a thief,' he said hotly.

'Except for pinching my necklace.'

'I *am* sorry. But it was so fascinating…' His eyes lit up. Clara's heart sank slightly – she could recognise when someone was about to talk about their hobby. At least it wasn't football.

'The technology on this world is very interesting,' the ambassador said. 'Not least because it's localised around one area. A strip of land—'

'Between the mountains and the sea,' said Clara. 'Varuz.'

He nodded. 'That's right. Now that in itself would be interesting, in that usually what happens is that technological advances get carried abroad and spread around, but that doesn't seem to have happened here. Then add to that the fact that I'm not clear how much of their technology still works, and from my short time there it's clear that the people of Varuz aren't clear either… It's all a great puzzle.'

'They seem to have known how it worked once,' Clara said. 'But the secrets got lost.'

'And sadly there's not much information about Varuz in my databanks,' the ambassador said. 'But from what I've been able to gather, the craft to make these devices – the lights, the weapons, whatever else there might still be there – this knowledge was in the hands of a privileged few. Only they were allowed to study and to make – and over the centuries they made huge advances.'

'What kind of advances?' Clara said.

'Well, there are stories that they got to the stars,' said the alien, 'but I haven't been able to find evidence that they did. You'd expect to find some record of them elsewhere… but then this place is a long way out. Perhaps they didn't meet anyone else while they were travelling. There are other stories too, about incredible weapons. Varuz was the great power on this world, once upon a time, thanks to its superior technology. But their influence waned, their knowledge disappeared, and only the artefacts remained.'

'Do we know what caused their decline?' asked Clara.

The alien shrugged. 'Could be anything. Overreached themselves. Economic collapse. Plague. The usual things.'

'And they left everything around for people to pick up…' Clara touched her pendant.

'And these were so well made that many of them continue to function,' the alien said. 'They must seem like magic now, to most ordinary people. But they're not. They're built. They're *crafted*. And that's what I want to study. Your pendant…' He gestured towards it. 'It will have some kind of purpose. I just haven't had the chance to find out what that is.'

Clara clasped her hand around the jewel. 'You know a lot about this.'

'It's not my main area of interest,' he said, 'but it's an interesting side line.'

'What do you do with all this stuff, when you have it?' Clara said. 'Do you sell it?'

'What?' He looked shocked. 'Didn't you hear me say? I'm a *collector*.'

'A collector. So you hide it all away in a vault somewhere?'

'I take care of it, yes,' he said. 'Under proper conditions.'

'I can guess.' Clara frowned. 'Seems a shame for it all to disappear like that.'

He looked almost childishly hurt. 'I look at my collection all the time, when I'm home,' he said. 'I take good care of it. I love every single piece.'

'All right, I believe you! So what's brought you here? You weren't after my pendant, were you? And you said that Varuz was just an interesting side line…' She sat back on her heels. 'I don't even know your name! I can't keep calling you "ambassador", can I? On account of you not being one.'

He smiled. 'No, I suppose not. My name is Emfil.' The last syllable was lengthened: *Em-feeeel*. 'And, no, it wasn't your pendant that brought me here, although, as I say, it's very interesting.'

Clara looked down at it uneasily. 'The Doctor said it was emitting some kind of energy.'

'It is. It's also stuffed with circuitry.'

'Is it?'

Emfil nodded. He reached over to his pack, and pulled out a gadget which Clara assumed was a scanner of some sort. He ran this over the jewel, and then showed Clara the image on the screen: a complex pattern of tiny wires and links, as intricate as the metalwork on the setting, and obviously engineered in some way.

'Definitely not frippery,' she murmured. 'So what does it do?'

Emfil shrugged. 'I've no idea. Didn't the Duchess say?'

Clara shook her head. 'She might not know herself, if what you said about lost secrets is true. She might think it's just a necklace.' She glanced at Emfil. 'But that isn't what brought you here, you said. So what did?'

Emfil looked very uncomfortable. 'I can't say.'

'Oh, come on,' Clara said. 'No secrets between fellow alien visitors to distant worlds who've accidentally got themselves banished by the local feudal lord.'

Emfil looked serious. 'You promise you won't laugh?'

Clara put her hand on the pendant. 'I swear upon my mysterious jewellery.'

'All right,' said Emfil. 'As long as you promise not to laugh.' His voice went quiet, and very serious. 'I'm looking for a treasure more precious than any other,' he said. 'A treasure with more legends and stories attached to it than any other.' His voice dropped so that she could barely hear. Clara leaned forward. 'It's called,' said Emfil, 'the Glamour.'

'The what?'

'The Glamour.'

Clara frowned.

Emfil leaned in eagerly. 'Have you heard something about it?'

'No,' said Clara. 'I thought you were going to say something else.'

My decision made, I took myself to my rooms, and contemplated the quest to which I had committed myself. Was this course folly? Would it only hasten the end of our dear land? To take away the knights at this stage... But having seen Aurelian standing alone, I knew that I could not have acted in any other way. I closed my eyes, but I was not allowed to rest for long, as soon enough there was a knock at the door. In a quiet voice, I summoned my visitor to come inside.

It was the Doctor. He came inside and sat down opposite me.

'Don't go,' he urged me. 'There's no purpose in you going – any of you. You have to believe me when I say that Grail doesn't exist. These knights – they're chasing a chimera, a mirage.'

'Doctor,' I said, 'you are a wise man, but in this you seem to be strangely blind. Whether the Grail exists or not does not matter.'

'Oh, Bernhardt! You're not listening—!'

'Doctor – now is the time for *you* to listen.' I

rested my hands flat upon my knees. 'This Grail – it is immaterial whether or not we can find this thing. What matters is that by taking on this quest, I have restored my lord's faith in me, and, in doing that, I have restored the confidence of his knights in him. And *that*, Doctor – that is a pearl beyond price.'

He was shaking his head.

'This quest,' I said, 'will hold us together for a little while longer, at least. You claim not to want war.'

'Of course I don't want war! You know full well I don't want that!'

'This may be the way to prevent Aurelian from taking battle to Conrad. He was set upon that course until Lancelot arrived. But if we are busy chasing…' I smiled at him. 'If we are busy chasing a mirage, we cannot waste ourselves waging war, can we?'

The Doctor contemplated my words. 'You're a wise man, Bernhardt.'

'I only speak the truth as I see it.'

'Hmm.' The Doctor had taken out his favourite toy, the long thin piece of metal, and he twisted it round in his hands. 'I suppose you might be right. Although what will happen when Aurelian finally realises that the Grail does not exist, I'm not entirely sure. What damage will that do to his knights' faith in him?'

'Perhaps by then we will have found the courage to face our end. Because the end is coming, Doctor. I know that, and I have long since made my peace with it. I hope that when it comes, I will have the courage to face it and to stand shoulder-to-shoulder with my lord, who is also my friend. And perhaps, on this quest, we might find *something* – some kind of fortitude, maybe, to bring back to the final battle.'

'That might be all you hope for, Bernhardt,' he said, 'but I don't surrender easily. I have to *understand*… These knights – who *are* they? Where have they come from?'

'You said they came from Clara's land,' I replied. 'Doctor, where is that, exactly?'

The Doctor waved his hands about. The device he was holding hummed and buzzed. 'Oh, you know, very far away, over the mountains and so on…'

'Do you mean from beyond the stars?'

He looked at me fiercely. 'What do you know about what lies beyond the stars?'

'You heard Aurelian,' I replied. 'There are stories that have come down to us through the centuries that say that the Lords of Varuz once walked amongst the stars.'

There was a pause. Then the Doctor said, 'That could be figurative.'

'It could indeed,' I said. 'Or it could be the simple truth. You forget that I have lived my whole life amongst devices the making of which I cannot comprehend,' I said. 'Lights that come on with the flick of a hand. Swords that burn. What else did our forefathers make? What voyages did they embark upon? Which strange worlds did they visit, as you now visit ours?'

He did not reply to any of this.

'It is clear to me that Clara – and you – come from a world very distant from my own,' I said. 'And now this Lancelot has arrived too. What has brought you here?'

'I keep saying this,' said the Doctor, 'but there was no Lancelot. No Holy Grail. Just stories…'

'And yet here he is. Might it be that the Grail, too, exists?'

'No,' he said. 'Emphatically not.' He sat frowning for a long while, the metal device spinning round and round in his hands. 'Still, I suppose I'd better come along with you. To keep an eye on things.'

My heart lightened considerably to hear this news. 'I would be very glad of your company on the road.'

He looked around my rooms, an ill-tempered expression on his place. 'I would have thought you'd be glad to get away. It's depressing here.' Perhaps he caught something passing across my face, for he frowned and said, 'Am I being rude again? Sorry. I suppose it was very nice once.'

'It is home,' I said, simply.

'I miss Clara!' he said. 'She always tells me when I'm being rude! I hope she's had the sense to go with the ambassador to Conrad.'

I laughed at that.

'What?' he said. 'What's funny?'

'For a wise man, Doctor, you can be very foolish.'

'I know that already. But how in particular am I being foolish now?'

'I do not know exactly who that man was,' I said, 'but he was certainly no ambassador from Conrad.'

'What makes you say that?'

'There were many clues,' I said. 'But chiefly – why would he be travelling alone? Where was his entourage?'

'Didn't he have a dangerous journey, though?' the Doctor said. 'Aren't there bandits, or something?'

'All the better to travel with companions then,' I replied. 'But there were other signs. He knew none of the forms of address, for example – and while I know that Conrad is a man of the people, even he takes the trouble to use the appropriate forms.'

'Perhaps it was meant as an insult,' the Doctor said.

'Doctor,' I said firmly, 'that man was no ambassador from Conrad.'

'All right, I'll take your word for it. So who was he? What was he doing here?'

'I have no idea. Looking for a Grail of his own, perhaps?'

'Clara…' he said. 'I sent her off with him…'

'She struck me as a young woman of great ability,' I said. 'If anyone can take our message to Conrad, I believe it will be her.'

'I hope so,' said the Doctor. 'But who was that man if not the ambassador? What did he want? And exactly how many people are there wandering around Varuz these days?'

Too many, I thought, and soon our company would be another.

'What did you think I meant?' asked Emfil. 'Is there some other treasure I should know about?'

'Don't worry,' said Clara. 'It's just a story. So tell me about the Glamour. What is it? Is it jewellery? Is that why you wanted a better look at my pendant?'

Emfil chewed his bottom lip. 'To be honest, Clara, I'm not sure…'

'Well, what does it look like? You must know what it looks like?'

Emfil was embarrassed. 'Not really, no…'

'OK,' said Clara. 'So how long have you been looking for the Glamour, exactly?'

'The whole of my adult life,' Emfil said wistfully.

'Lifespans may vary,' said Clara. 'How long is that?'

'About ninety-seven—' The word that followed went on for a good few seconds, and Clara wasn't sure that all the sounds in it were within her hearing range.

'I don't have enough consonants to say that back to you,' she said, 'but ninety-seven sounds like it could be a lot of them. So you've been looking for this thing for ninety-seven whatever-they-ares and you don't know what it looks like? Have you thought you might be in the wrong job?'

'Any really important task is worth it,' Emfil said, huffily.

'It sounds a bit pie in the sky to me.'

Emfil looked up anxiously. 'Pie in the sky?'

'Figure of speech,' said Clara. 'Forget it. So what brought you here? Do you have a lead?'

Emfil looked at her suspiciously. 'You're very interested in my business all of a sudden. Why do you want to know?'

'All right,' said Clara. 'Listen. I'm not interested in your Glamour, whatever it is. Really, anything that takes more than ninety-seven penny-whistle-and-kazoos to find – I'm just not interested. Do I look like a patient woman? I can hardly stand waiting for my morning cup of tea. I'm asking because you're the only person around here who doesn't want to come at me with a burny sword, and I'm trying to be nice. So what brought you to this world?'

Emfil was still wary, but he said, 'There are other people pursuing it. I heard they'd come this way.'

'Others?' Clara laughed out loud. 'How many aliens *are* there on this world right now?'

'I don't know. They might not be here at all. It's not a precise science. I might be a star system or two out.'

'Ah.'

'So – I've explained my business,' said Emfil. 'What about you? What brought you here – you and your master?'

'He is not my master, father, boyfriend, or anything else,' Clara said firmly. 'Is that clear?'

'All right, all right!' Emfil flapped his hands in a soothing gesture. 'Sorry!'

'We're friends, OK? Why is it so difficult for people to get that? We're friends, and we're travellers. Sightseers. We wanted to see somewhere nice.' Clara looked around the mountainside. 'And bits of it *are* nice – very nice – and bits of it are just plain weird, and on top of all that there's going to be a war, probably, and I thought you were the means by which I could do something to stop that, but it turns out that you're a stamp collector or whatever the space equivalent of that is, and now I don't have anyone to take me to Conrad but I'm going to have to try anyway because the Doctor asked me to, and somehow I always end up doing what the Doctor asks me to, even when I think it's a terrible idea. Anyway, that's who I am.'

'Sorry to disappoint,' said Emfil, in a rather subdued voice.

'I'll get over it. So where are you going now?'

'I haven't decided,' he said. 'I suppose I could always go back to my ship...' He didn't look too happy at that idea. 'But I've come an awfully long way...'

'And you don't want to leave without discovering whether the Glamour is here or not. Fair enough. Well, I'm going over the border,' Clara said decisively. 'To Conrad's country. You're welcome to come with me if you like. As far as I can tell, it's a lot richer over there, so there's probably more of the kind of stuff that you're interested in. There might be some news about the Glamour too.'

'Hmm…' Emfil didn't look convinced. 'My readings did suggest that I needed to be in this part of the world…'

'Long way to come to leave empty-handed. And, besides,' she added cheerfully, 'don't forget that we've been banished from Varuz. And sunrise has been and gone. We'd better get moving, or else…' She waved an imaginary laser-sword about. 'Could get hot.'

'All right,' said Emfil, reluctantly. 'I suppose it wouldn't do any harm. I don't want to get mixed up in anything unpleasant, though.'

'Er, you're the one who turned up in a war zone pretending to be an ambassador.' Clara felt obliged to point this out.

'I didn't know it was a war zone!'

'You didn't do your research, then.'

'It's hard to do research,' he said sulkily, 'when the world you're visiting doesn't have a galactic presence.'

'So you just turned up and hoped you'd get away with pretending to be an ambassador?'

He shrugged. 'It's worked in the past. Nobody expects an ambassador to reveal *too* much. They expect you to be playing your cards close to your chest.'

Clara shook her head. 'Got to admire your nerve,' she said. 'Your bad luck they really were expecting one this time, I suppose. We had the same problem, now I think about it.'

Having made the decision to carry on in each other's company, they set off again up the mountain path, trading stories of places they'd been and sights they'd seen. Now that he was no longer concealing his identity, Emfil turned out to be quite entertaining company. If you had to be banished, Clara thought, there were worse people to be banished with than someone who had seen so many interesting places. Still, the journey was tough going, and increasingly so, as the path led them higher, and became narrower and more treacherous underfoot.

After scrabbling along a particularly rough section that led them round the curve of the mountain they came out, unexpectedly, into a round hollow in the mountain. There was a small clutch of wiry bushes over towards one side and, with a shock, Clara realised there were people lying there. She froze, expecting them to jump up from their hiding place and approach them. But nobody moved. She took a cautious step towards them.

'No,' said Emfil, suddenly, his voice very sharp.

'Don't go any closer.' He swallowed. 'Let me go and look.'

He came back after a few minutes, visibly shaken. 'Four of them,' he said. 'All dead.'

Clara shuddered. 'How?'

'I think lasers must have been involved – No, don't go and look! It's horrible.' He took a deep breath, and then pulled out his scanner again. 'There's something I want to check, though.'

'What?' Clara asked, trying not to look over at the bushes.

'The symbols on their clothes,' said Emfil. 'I think I recognise them.' After a few minutes fiddling with the device, he nodded. 'Yes,' he said. 'These people – they're from Conrad's country. Clara, you know who this probably is?'

'The ambassador and his party,' she said. 'This is terrible. Who would *do* this?'

They heard a noise behind them: the crunch of footsteps on the rocky path leading their way. They looked round for somewhere to hide, but there was nowhere – only the path leading out of the hollow up the mountain. Even if they went that way, it would not take long for their pursuer to catch up with them, and the narrow pathways would put them at disadvantage.

'Stuck,' said Emfil. 'This trip is turning out not to

be one of my favourites.'

'And I think we're about to find out who killed the ambassador,' Clara replied. 'Let's hope they're prepared to let a couple of stray travellers go on their way.'

'But we know where the bodies are buried!'

'Play dumb,' she said. 'It usually works.'

Chapter

7

The footsteps had stopped. 'Come on,' muttered Clara. 'Put us out of our misery...'

'Don't say that!' said Emfil. 'I don't want to die.'

'They might not kill,' said Clara.

'We're witnesses to murder!'

'This might not be the murderer—'

'We're in the middle of nowhere! Who else is it going to be?'

Fair point, Clara thought. But who would have murdered the ambassador? Was there anyone who would gain from that? Conrad wouldn't; neither would Guena. Aurelian? Perhaps, if he wanted to send a message back to Conrad, but for all his flaws, Aurelian didn't strike her as the kind of man to kill in an underhand fashion. He would prefer the open field, the sword in his hand, riding towards the enemy. Could this have been the act of one of his followers, acting on their own initiative?

'Perhaps they've come for us,' said Emfil, and gave a low moan. 'Oh, how could we have been so stupid? This was always the plan, wasn't it? Send us off into the middle of nowhere and then send someone after us to murder us.'

'No,' said Clara firmly. 'The Doctor wouldn't let them do that.'

'The Doctor isn't here!'

The crunch of footsteps began again; much closer now. Then a head appeared over the edge of the hollow – a dark head of hair – and a man lowered himself down to join them.

It was Lord Mikhail.

He was no longer dressed in his finery, but for his long journey. He had laid his hands upon a sword somehow, Clara noted, although she doubted that Aurelian would have let him keep one. Perhaps he had friends in the city, who had armed him secretly before he left. It struck Clara that for a man who had been sent away from his home, he seemed to be much more at his ease here in the mountains than he had been in the city.

'If it was at all your intent to be quiet,' Mikhail said, walking towards them with his hand around the hilt of his sword, 'I can assure you that you were failing. Were you not concerned that Aurelian may have sent soldiers to make sure you left?' He looked around and then, inevitably, he saw the bodies. He recoiled, and murmured something under his breath.

Clara said, 'Are you responsible for that?'

He looked at her angrily. 'What kind of man do you think I am?'

'I don't know,' said Clara, honestly. 'I've only ever seen you losing your temper with your uncle. I know you've been banished. And so you might be wanting to find a way to buy your way back into Aurelian's favour.'

'I do not want his favour,' Mikhail said. 'I want nothing from him. And if this was the price…' He shook his head. 'Of course I did not do this evil thing – and nor, for that matter, do I believe that Aurelian would do this. He may not be a wise man, but neither is he a murderer.'

He took a deep breath, and then crossed over to the bodies, and began to search them. Clara was horrified. 'Leave them alone!' she cried. 'Isn't what's happened to them bad enough?'

'There may be messages,' Mikhail said. 'And, besides, I would like to have them lie peacefully rather than this. I would like them to have some dignity in death.'

'I'm sorry,' Clara said, in a quieter voice. Perhaps there was more to Mikhail than she had so far seen. 'Can I do anything?'

He nodded, so she helped him move and then cover the bodies.

When this was all done, Mikhail stood and sighed. Emfil, at his request, had gone to fetch water, and Mikhail and Clara washed, thoroughly. 'There should be a burial,' Mikhail said. 'Words said over them to help them to rest. But I cannot do that here. We must go on. We will tell Conrad's people where to find them, and hope that, in time, the right thing can be done.'

'Tell Conrad's people?' said Emfil.

'That is where we are all heading is it not?' Mikhail said. He looked thoughtfully at Emfil. 'You, sir, how did you survive this massacre?'

'Eh?' said Emfil.

'Were you not with the others of your party when they were attacked? Or did they defend you while you made your escape? It was brave of them if so.'

Clara realised that the young lord was still labouring under the mistaken belief that Emfil was the ambassador.

'For that matter, why did you not bring your whole party to Varuz?' Mikhail said. 'Aurelian likes pomp. He would surely have been impressed. You might not have been sent away so peremptorily.'

'Yeah,' said Clara. 'You know, we should probably explain something.'

'I'm not the ambassador,' said Emfil. 'I'm just a visitor. Sorry.'

Clara, waiting for Mikhail to become angry, was surprised. Against, expectation, the young man started to laugh. 'So my uncle was duped, was he? Perhaps it is mischievous of me, but I cannot help but be amused.' He quickly sobered. 'Still, we must bring this sad news to Conrad, and it may not be good for Varuz when he learns that his messengers have died here.'

'Are you sure that going to Conrad is a good idea?' said Clara. 'You're part of the royal family of Varuz – the last one, apart from Guena. Isn't that right?'

'That's right,' said Mikhail. 'But Conrad will see me, I am sure of that. Aurelian does not want my service. So I shall offer it instead to Conrad, and with it make an offer of peace.'

'Or he might take you hostage,' said Clara. 'Try to sell you back, or get some concession from Aurelian.'

'He would be misjudging my value to Aurelian if he did,' Mikhail said. He turned to Emfil. 'If you are not from Conrad, then who are you? Why are you here in Varuz?'

Clara was expecting some kind of prevarication, but to her surprise, Emfil was more or less honest. 'I'm a collector,' he said. 'I'm interested in beautiful things.'

Mikhail frowned. 'Did you come to rob us?'

'What?' Emfil was shocked. 'No, I always pay good prices! In local scrip, too.'

'More or less,' Clara muttered, but she didn't push the issue.

Mikhail sighed. 'Money is not what Varuz needs now,' he said. 'But that is no matter.'

'It was all a misunderstanding,' said Emfil, humbly. 'I arrived in the city and before I knew it I was swept up and presented to the Duke. I didn't know what to do. I didn't want to embarrass anyone.'

'To be fair,' said Clara, 'that sort of happened to us too.'

Mikhail smiled. 'Then I shall judge you on your future actions, and not those of the past. But this is a strange coincidence! You are not the only one to have come to Varuz looking for lost treasure, although in truth we have little in the way of riches left. They would be better travelling to Conrad's country, I think, but they seem most certain of their quest, and set upon travelling through Varuz. Aurelian is enamoured, I understand, and eager to help—'

'What do you mean?' said Clara. 'Who are they?'

'A company of knights,' Mikhail said, 'led by an old captain going by the name of Lancelot.'

'*Lancelot?*' Clara stared at him in amazement.

'He says they have come to find the Grail.'

'All right,' said Clara, 'this has gone *weird*. Being banished is pretty weird, and then,' she glanced at Emfil, 'the rest of it – but Lancelot? The Grail? Are you sure, Mikhail?'

'It seems that this knight and his quest are known to you, lady,' Mikhail said. 'Do I guess right?'

'Well, sort of,' Clara said. 'But Lancelot is a story – the Grail too. From my country.' She turned to Emfil. 'It's a story about lost treasure. Something mystical and unknown.'

Emfil understood. 'This could be what I'm looking for, but under a different name…'

Mikhail had been listening closely to all this, and with interest. 'It seems that there is much to learn here. Your country, you say, Clara – and I would like to hear more about that, I think. And you, sir – ' he turned to Emfil – 'I would hear more about your quest too. But the way back to the palace is closed to you. If you return, Aurelian will have you killed. And we cannot linger here…' He sighed. 'We should go. We are still some distance from the border and we cannot risk remaining in Varuz much longer. I do not know whether Aurelian has had me followed. Let us go. Conrad will help.'

They scrambled out of the hollow and on up the path. Clara looked back at where the bodies lay. A nasty suspicion was growing in her mind. 'He *might*,' she muttered. 'Or he might finish us for good.'

Although I was no longer living in fear of my life, I knew that Aurelian would now have people watching me. I barely dared to set foot out of my rooms, unless on some matter clearly related to my imminent journey, and I most certainly did not dare approach my lady directly. But speak to her I must. And so I took out the mirror, and I sat before it, and, reaching into a drawer, I took out the little silver ring with the emerald that had been my lady's gift to me so many years ago.

'Guena,' I whispered. 'I am here. Lady, do you hear me? Will you speak to me?'

The polished surface of the mirror shimmered. I had used this device many times over the years, but still it was marvellous to me. How had our ancestors fashioned such wonders? What craft lay behind them? And after the wonder came the sorrow: that all the skill and knowledge that had filled the world with such phenomena were lost, and only we remained, the sad inheritors, blundering around using tools that we did not understand.

And then there she was, my beloved lady, the last of her line save one. 'Bernhardt,' she said softly. 'My love. Have they harmed you at all?'

I shook my head. 'No, and indeed I have had every aid to help me depart on my quest.' I gave a soft laugh. 'One might think Aurelian is eager for me to depart. But what about you, my love? Has he spoken to you since?'

'No, no, I have not seen him. He is with this captain – Lancelot.'

'Aye, he is much taken with him,' I said. 'I less so.'

'And I am not taken at all. Bernhardt,' she said, 'I understand why you have taken this quest upon yourself, but do you think this journey is wise at this time?'

'What other option is there?' I said. 'If I do not go, the knights will split. There will be no defence against Conrad. And I shall be sitting under lock and key when his army arrives—' I stopped, suddenly, for I had heard the crack of a floorboard behind me.

'Well, well, well,' said a familiar voice. 'What do we have here?'

'Doctor,' I said, with some asperity. 'How is it that you, of all men, remain able to move freely around this palace?'

He shrugged. 'Well, for all that's happened, Aurelian wouldn't dare lay a hand on a holy man.'

'Doctor,' said Guena, 'you are no more a holy man than I.'

'Oh, mirror, mirror, on the wall,' said the Doctor, 'who is the fairest of them all? You know,' he said, and he fell into a seat beside me, 'if I'd known sooner that you two wanted to talk to each other, I could have done something about it. Still, you seem to be on top of things.' He tapped the side of the mirror. 'What is this, exactly? And don't say a mirror. Don't say a magic mirror either. I'll only get cross. Crosser. What is it, Guena?'

'Who knows?' said my lady. 'I certainly do not. My father, the Duke, taught me how to use it. He learned from his father, as did his before him, and so on back through the centuries. The secrets of its making are long lost, but our forebears built well, and I have never known this device to fail me.'

The Doctor lifted out his metal wand, and waved it across the mirror. 'Oh, I see,' he said. 'That's quite clever. You know, ordinarily this kind of thing uses an incredible amount of energy. You see it sucking up coal, or gas, or sunlight, or whatever it is that's par for the course. But this thing – it seems hardly to be using anything at all, and whatever it's using, I just can't tell…' He frowned. 'But, you know, there's no such thing as a free lunch, particularly when it comes to powering sophisticated technological devices. I wonder what your clever forebears did exactly. How does this thing *work*?'

He leaned back in towards it, waving around his little piece of metal, and it seemed to me that he might well begin to dismantle the mirror before my lady and I had had our chance to speak.

'Doctor,' I said. 'Guena and I have very little time, and a great deal to discuss.'

'What?' He looked up. 'Oh, sorry, yes. I'll stick around, if you don't mind. I might have a few ideas.'

And so we held our hurried council. 'I think it is great folly,' said my lady, 'to remove our knights from their positions. If Conrad moves against us, it will prove ruinous. Bernhardt,' she said, 'you have won back the Duke's favour. Do you think that he might be dissuaded from sending the knights away?'

'Lady,' I said, 'I have not won back his favour. I have merely brought him some consolation in his despair. It is Lancelot who holds his affection now.'

'Lancelot,' she said, and almost snarled at the name. 'I do not trust him. I do not trust any of his company. I would not be surprised if they had come from Conrad, and were part of plot to make us leave the city undefended.'

'If it's a plot, it's an elaborate one,' said the Doctor. 'And how have they heard of the Grail? Of Lancelot? Why would they use that story instead of one from your own history that meant something to you? Something about finding the secrets of your own lost gadgets.' He shook his head. 'No, these knights must have come from Clara's world, or, at the very least, have visited it at some point in its history. But when? And how?'

'I shall leave these matters to you, Doctor, since they seem to concern you greatly,' said my lady. 'The defence of Varuz is my concern.'

'And, as you say, with the knights away, the city stands defenceless,' I said. 'Is there news yet of Mikhail?'

'Not yet,' she said. 'I have sent him several messages, but have heard nothing in reply.'

'And has there been any news of Clara, Doctor?' I said.

'No, nothing. Still on her way to Conrad, I hope.'

'We can only hope that Conrad receives no news

of this quest,' said Guena. 'If he learns that the city is now undefended, he will surely move against us.'

'Or perhaps he might pursue the Grail himself,' I said. 'If only we knew what it was! If it was a weapon of kind – even if only a symbol – we might guess whether or not Conrad might choose to chase it.'

'And if he did, he would be wasting his time,' said the Doctor. 'Because – as I may have said before – *the Grail doesn't exist.*'

'And yet here is Lancelot,' I said, 'and here are his knights, and we leave at first light.'

The party of three, as they were now, continued their trek up the mountain. As they walked, Mikhail explained the route that they were going to take: up, and up, and then the narrow path reached a high valley. They would cross this and, once again, find a path that would lead them to the high pass over the mountain and then down into Conrad's country.

'What we will find there, I do not know,' he admitted. 'Conrad has kept the passes closed for many a long year now. We have spent many men trying to force them open. And I fear we may not be left in peace even on this side of the border. While we walk the mountain's paths there is little in the way of cover, and whoever murdered the ambassador might still be close. Those people were not long dead.'

Clara shuddered. It was not pleasant to think that the whole time she and Emfil had been travelling, danger had most likely been very close. For the moment, however, they walked on undisturbed and, as they went, and she and Mikhail talked, Clara gained more of an understanding of the young man: his frustration at having been side-lined; his growing belief that Aurelian was not the man Varuz needed at this time; and that his policies were in danger of bringing down a bloody revenge upon Varuz. As he spoke, she found her respect for him growing too. Away from the court, he was not the angry and alienated young man that she had seen, but proved more reflective and shrewd.

'You must understand, Clara, that, once upon a time, Varuz ruled the world.'

Clara put her hand around the jewel of Guena's pendant. 'Because of your superior technology.'

'Because of the devices we had at our command we were able to rule many of the lands that Conrad now calls his own.' Mikhail frowned. 'But most of our devices are now lost, except for the odd piece in the hands of some of the lords, given as gifts.' He nodded at the pendant. 'And some other tools that endure, like the lamps that blaze through the city or the swords that some of the knights still bear. But the resentment arising from our rule is still very much alive, as if our dominion had ended only yesterday. It rankles still with Conrad.'

'Nobody likes an overlord,' said Clara. 'Particularly one who has all the best toys. But couldn't Conrad just leave you alone behind your mountains, until everything broke and the lights went out?'

'Leave us alone? To discover our lost secrets and wage war on the world again? For that, I imagine, is what Conrad believes we will do – although we do not have the power or the means. But if that was my belief… I am not sure that if I was in his place, I would leave us alone, Clara.' They walked on in silence for a while, and at length he smiled. 'So,' he said, 'this is my inheritance – such as it is – and even from that I have been dispossessed.'

Behind them, Emfil sighed. He was clearly not enjoying the walk. Mikhail studied him thoughtfully for a few moments, and then turned to Clara. Softly, he said, 'Do you trust this one? He claims that his embassy was all a misunderstanding, but from what I saw of him, he seemed to take advantage of our mistake.'

Clara thought about this for a while. 'I don't think he'd betray us,' she said. 'But I don't think he's the kind of person to take one for the team.'

'What do you mean?'

'Putting it bluntly? I think he might run away from trouble. And I don't really blame him,' she said. 'This isn't his war, after all. He turned up looking to buy some pretty things, and has found himself walking up a mountain with some bloodthirsty killers at his back. He's not a soldier, or an adventurer, Mikhail. He's just someone quite ordinary.'

Mikhail nodded his understanding, then looked at the path rising up ahead. 'Keep heart!' he called back to Emfil. 'Soon we reach the high valley! We can rest there!'

The sun rose overhead, and they walked on. After an hour or two, they realised that there were others on the path ahead, coming their way. Mikhail, drawing his sword, ordered Clara and Emfil to stand behind him. 'Do not be afraid,' he said, but Clara couldn't think of anyone likely to be here that she would want to see. Messengers from Aurelian, sent to kill them? Scouts from Conrad, to prevent their crossing the mountains? Or the murderers of the ambassador, keen to dispose of any possible witnesses? She stood behind Mikhail and wished that she had brought a knife, or something with which she could defend herself, or that her necklace might suddenly start throwing around some death rays. That, she thought, was exactly what she needed right now.

As she watched, six men came into view, all armed, and dressed in uniforms. 'Oh,' she murmured, recognising the colours. They were the same as those she had seen on the dead bodies.

'Yes,' said Mikhail. 'These men are from Conrad.'

The group stopped, a few feet away, and their leader called out to Mikhail. 'Put down your sword, sorcerer. Even that foul device won't protect you against so many of us.'

To Clara's surprise, Mikhail obeyed, sheathing the sword again. 'I mean no harm, sir,' he said. 'I hope to cross into your country, and I bring with me two ordinary people. We have all been sent away from Varuz. We hope to make a home amongst you.'

The soldiers fell into position around them, three at the front, three at the back, and led them on up the path.

'Mikhail,' Clara whispered, 'are they spies?'

'No,' he whispered back, 'spies would not be in uniform. A scouting party, perhaps?' He frowned. 'But again, why the uniforms? Why not camouflaged?'

The soldier closest to them tapped Mikhail on

the shoulder. 'No talking. Follow us.'

They went on up the path in silence, and, coming through a narrow gap between sheer cliffs, they entered the valley that Mikhail had described. There, to Clara's amazement, they saw a busy encampment: more than a hundred great tents flying various devices that she had begun to recognise. 'Those colours,' she said. 'They're Conrad's, aren't they?'

'Yes,' said Mikhail. 'And we are not yet in Conrad's country.'

'This is it, isn't it?' she said. 'The invasion. It's already started.'

'It seems so,' said Mikhail.

'So we're too late,' she said. 'War is here.'

'Perhaps not,' said Mikhail. 'But there's a saying in Varuz. It's a long way from the mountains to the sea.'

They were hushed again, and led on. The encampment was bustling; men working at their gear or with their horses; messengers running to and fro – all was busy, and excited, as if some great project was under way. The conquest of Varuz.

They came to a great tent at the centre of the camp. Two guards were outside, but, at a word from the leader of their group, they stood back to let them through. Inside, a great table covered in maps took most of the space; several men and women, armed and uniformed, were gathered around it, in debate. As they came in, their discussion stopped. The oldest of the group, one of the men, looked up from the maps. 'What is this?' He sounded displeased. 'Did I not say we were not to be interrupted?'

Before the guards could speak, Mikhail approached the speaker, and bowed low. 'Lord Conrad,' he said. 'I come to you in the hope of peace.'

Chapter
8

Mikhail was met with silence. And then Conrad began to laugh. He turned to his generals. 'In peace,' he said. 'The heir to Varuz comes to *me* in peace! Did we ever think that we would live to see this day?' Turning back to Mikhail, he said, 'It is too late to look for a settlement, sir. You see that I am here in Varuz, and have come here unmolested. You see my army. What terms could you offer to me?' He gestured to the guards, but Mikhail spoke again, quickly.

'I have information for you, sir. Things have changed in Varuz, and Aurelian has a new scheme, one that you could not have planned for.'

Conrad hesitated, and then he dropped his hand and the guards drew back. He walked up to Mikhail and, standing before him, studied the young man very closely. Clara shivered at the look: it was calculating, almost predatory. Conrad, she thought, was proving something of a disappointment. She doubted she could make Guena's case to this man.

'So you've turned traitor, have you, Mikhail?' Conrad said. 'It was only a matter of time. Aurelian should have ruled from behind the throne, rather than taking it as his own, I always thought.'

Mikhail, to give him his due, was not flinching or cowering under such close scrutiny. He had several inches advantage on Conrad, in terms of height, although the older man was powerfully built and strong. 'I do not disagree, sir. But that is a discussion for another day.' He looked behind him, to where Emfil and Clara stood. 'We have a strange tale to tell you, sir, my friends and I. You need to hear what we have to say. A company of knights has come to Aurelian's aid, and their presence in Varuz may well alter your plans. Will you hear what we have to tell you?'

Conrad looked back at his generals, who all nodded their own interest. So Conrad went and sat in a high-backed chair, and gestured to the three travellers to come before him. 'Speak,' he said, and Mikhail launched into an account of the arrival of Lancelot and his men at the Great Hall, of their quest for the Grail, and how Aurelian had commanded his own knights to join the quest. Conrad sat listening intently. 'But what is it, this thing, this Grail?' he said. 'A weapon?'

'Of its nature, I know very little,' admitted Mikhail, 'although its power is such that it has kept these knights in search of it for years. But my friend here –' he nodded to Emfil – 'may know a little more.'

Conrad turned to Emfil, who, with much stammering and stuttering, explained something about his search for the Glamour. At Clara's whispered instruction, he skipped the part about being from another planet. Conrad surely wouldn't believe that and he might doubt the rest of their story as result. And, besides, Conrad seemed to have the conquering bug. Clara wasn't keen on putting the idea of whole new worlds in front of him. When Emfil finished, Conrad sat for a while, his chin resting in his hand, deep in thought.

'These are fascinating tales,' he said at last. 'I must admit that the temptation is very strong to chase whatever Aurelian is chasing, and to beat him to this object.' He leaned back in his chair, and stretched out, like a lion taking its ease in the afternoon sun. 'But the simple truth is, I do not care a fig for grails or glamours.'

One of the generals stepped forward. 'Sir,' she

said, 'this might not be wise—'

'Fear not, Lucinda,' he said. 'I'm not a fool! This seems a distraction to me, and an unnecessary one. But I do understand the significance of symbols. If this quest for the Grail will unite Aurelian's knights and the people of Varuz behind him, then I will do what can to prevent him.'

The general stood back, satisfied. But Clara wanted some answers. She had come hoping that she might persuade Conrad to listen to Guena's petition, but she saw now that this was a waste of time. His hatred of Varuz ran too deep, and informed every decision that he made.

'Why do you want Varuz so much?' she said. 'I suppose it's pretty enough, or some of it is, and the walking holidays must be excellent. I know my calf muscles won't be the same again after all this. But it's falling apart. Why bring an army all this way? It's like cutting a loaf of bread with… Well, with a laser-sword. Why not just leave it be? Leave Varuz to quietly crumble?'

'I rule from the eastern sea to the mountains,' Conrad said. 'I rule all the wide green lands beneath the sun. Except Varuz.'

'So what you're saying is that you don't like a gap in your collection?' Clara shook her head. 'Emfil, I thought you were wasting your time, but this is something else.' She turned back to Conrad. 'You know, wanting to have everything is not a great reason to start a war. In fact, it's a pretty terrible reason. Probably the worst one out there.'

Conrad was starting to look impatient. 'I do not know who you are, lady, but I think you know very little of our history. Varuz was the conqueror once. Over many years, we have pushed them back and we will continue to do so until their influence is washed away.'

'That sounds unpleasant for Varuz,' Clara said. 'And I'll confess I don't know much about your history, but I'm fairly certain there's nobody alive there now who was responsible for conquering you. And, anyway, you can't keep fighting wars because of the last one.'

'There will be no more wars after this one,' said Conrad.

'I've heard that before,' said Clara.

'There needn't be war now,' Conrad said, 'if Aurelian will hear my embassy and surrender his rule.'

The three travellers looked uneasily at each other.

'Sir,' said Mikhail. 'We have bad news—'

'Your embassy,' said Clara, 'isn't going to reach Aurelian.'

Mikhail put his hand upon her arm. 'I should be the one to explain,' he said, and he did, describing how they had found the bodies on the hillside, and explaining their unhappy end. The others there gasped in horror, but Conrad remained coldly in control.

'Who did this?' he said. 'Did Aurelian order this?'

'Sir, we expected your embassy, but we had no knowledge of when he might arrive and what route he might take,' said Mikhail. 'We did not know enough to waylay him.'

'And, anyway, Aurelian wouldn't do that,' Clara said. 'Well, he wouldn't!' she said again, when she heard muttering around the room. 'He's prepared to meet you in battle, but he wouldn't send assassins to kill your ambassador.'

'You speak highly of Aurelian,' said Conrad.

'I think he's made a lot of mistakes, and I think he's mistaken if he thinks he can hold you and your army off, but I don't think he would do something as brutal and as underhand as that. Look,' said Clara, 'I don't have any vested interest in all this. I don't want land, or riches, or jewels, or titles. I just don't want to see you all killing each other, and I particularly don't want to see ordinary people hurt, because it's usually ordinary people who get hurt when lords and generals start a war with each other. I'm just telling it to you straight.'

'That,' said Conrad, 'is not always an appealing quality.' He turned to Mikhail. 'Nevertheless, I am prepared to accept your word, lord, that Aurelian did not order this massacre.'

'You have my word,' said Mikhail. 'And I am no favourite of Aurelian's.'

'That I certainly know,' said Conrad. 'Yes, I can accept that Aurelian would not be duplicitous in this way. How true that is of the rest of his court, I am not sure.'

Clara flushed at this, thinking of her own scheming with Bernhardt and Guena.

'I see that the young lady, at least, has some idea of what I mean,' Conrad said. 'Aurelian is not perhaps informed of all that happens in his halls. But if Aurelian did not order this murder, then who might? Who could have killed these people?'

One of the generals spoke. 'There are many bandits in this country. Aurelian has struggled to sustain his rule across his lands.'

'It's only falling apart because you're barricading them in,' Clara pointed out. 'You know, I wouldn't be surprised if you ordered the murder of your ambassador yourself so that you had an excuse to invade—'

'Er, Clara,' whispered Emfil. 'Is this such a good

idea? I thought you were supposed to be, well, you know, trying to broker peace—'

There was anger around the room at Clara's words, and Conrad, looking very coolly at her, said, 'I shall forgive you that since you say that you know very little about the history of these lands. Do you know what kind of master Varuz was? A cruel one that used its superior strength and knowledge to crush the rest of the world so that its nobles could lead luxurious lives. Even now, the Duke uses the remnants of their power to attack us in our lands. Sudden explosions in our towns. Buildings turned to rubble. People killed and maimed—'

Mikhail intervened. 'Sir,' he said, 'I know nothing of this, but I know you would not lie, and for the harm done to your people by mine, I am sorry. Had I been Duke, it would not have happened with my cognizance. But all of this must end,' he went on. 'You and I, sir, we must stop all this. None of us is served by this.'

Mikhail turned to address the generals too.

'Aurelian represents the old order, looking back to a lost past that can never be regained, and which we should not want to see again. Those days are gone and the secrets of Varuz are gone with them. But there is no future for any of us in war, sir. Not for your country, not for what remains of mine, and not for all the green lands beneath the sun. Someone must be willing to look towards the future. Someone must be willing to end this impasse.' Stepping forwards, he knelt before Conrad. 'I am the heir to Varuz, sir. And I offer you my service. I will find you this Grail, this Glamour, if that is what you want.'

'Mikhail,' said Clara. 'I'm not sure this is a good idea…'

But Conrad was highly amused. 'You begin with an offer of peace and then give me an offer of service! Perhaps, if we talk a little longer, you will give me the keys to the city!' Then, rising from his seat, he held out his hands, and helped the young man to stand. 'I make light of your offer, which is unfair of me. You are a brave man, I think,' he said, 'and a wise one. I accept your service. But as for this Grail?' He smiled wolfishly. 'I have another task in mind for you, Mikhail.'

We left the city in the early morning, and I will admit that I was unsure whether I would see my home and my lady again. Where would this quest take us, in the end? If such a thing as the Grail did indeed exist, I had heard tell of nothing like it in all the lands between the mountains and the sea. Yes, we had tales of quests, of objects that were desired and lost and found and then discovered to no longer be desired in the same way – but are such tales not universal? Do they not speak to every human heart? For they speak to us of our follies, of the limits of our self-knowledge, but they also speak of the necessity of hope. I do not believe there is a land beneath the sun or a world spinning round a star that does not tell such tales. But an object of such mystery as the Grail? That I had not heard of before, and to know that it came from a distant world only confused me further. Why would it have come to Varuz, and by what means? Did our fathers indeed voyage amongst the stars? Their powers were extraordinary and their appetites mighty. Could they have visited Clara's home, once upon a time, and other worlds too? Did they bring back with them the relics of other worlds? Were they plunderers, our forefathers, gatherers-up of the wealth and treasures of others? That was a hard thing to think on.

But such thoughts consumed me as I rode through the city, and the rest of the company too seemed caught up in their own reveries, for we rode in silence. As we passed, however, cheers rose up at our passing, and sometimes even songs that instructed us to have heart, to be brave in the way that only the people of Varuz knew how to be. I saw us through the eyes of these witnesses, and thought that we must seem a very strange band. Lancelot and his grim knights were at the fore; behind them, I led a company of knights, the flower of Varuz. The Doctor rode beside me. The gates stood open, and we filed through. Beyond the city walls a great dais had been raised, and there Aurelian waited for us. We halted our progress and gathered around to hear him.

And such a speech he gave! Hearing him, my heart was filled again with great love for this man, companion of my youth and manhood, my Duke, lord of the land that I loved best. He spoke to us of Varuz, our home, and its greatness. He spoke to us of the charge that fell upon us: to bring aid to Lancelot and his men in their quest and in so doing, bring honour and renown to Varuz. Beside him stood his Duchess, Guena, and throughout the speech she and I were careful to make sure that our eyes never met.

When at last Aurelian finished, we cried out his name, *Aurelian!* and we cried the name of our home, *Varuz!* and then we set forth again. As the road bent away from the city, I turned to look back one last time, and I saw Guena, standing alone. She lifted her hand. *Farewell.*

For some time, I could do little more than make

myself ride on. But at length, I found my voice again, and I turned to my companion. 'Tell me, Doctor,' I said, 'about the tales that came from Clara's world. What became of the knights that rode upon the Quest? Did they find what they were looking for? Did they find their Holy Grail?'

He did not reply at once, and I wondered if he had heard me, but at length he sighed. 'The Grail could only be seen if a person was pure at heart – if they had led a pure life.'

I smiled at that. 'Can such a person exist?'

'In stories, yes,' he replied. 'And so it was in the case of this story. One of the knights, Galahad, had lived a pure life. He was courageous, and gentle, and courteous, and brave.'

'Now I know we are in a story,' I said. 'No such perfect knight could exist.'

'Galahad travelled in search of the Grail, and he came at last to a waste land. All that was left there was a ruined castle, and in the castle lived a wounded king. Inside the castle was the Grail.'

'And what happened when he saw it, Doctor?'

'He died, Bernhardt. He died, happy.'

I pondered this tale for a while, which seemed to me amongst the saddest that I had heard. Was any vision of perfection worth one's life? 'And what about Lancelot?' I said. 'Did he see the Grail?'

'Lancelot,' he said, 'was in love with Arthur's wife. And she was in love with him. Because of this, Lancelot never saw the Grail as anything other a dream – and even then, it was a blur.' He looked at me keenly. 'Was this failure? I'm not sure. Perhaps it was better to have loved the Queen and been loved in return, than to have touched the Holy Grail. But who am I to say?'

'And Arthur? What happened to him?'

'He died, of course, in battle. All kings die, in the end, and their kingdoms fall to ruin.'

I looked back again, but the road had bent away, and the city was lost in the misty dawn. My heart was heavy. I did not believe that I would find any grail on this journey, because I left behind me what I loved most of all. We rode on into wilder country, where the ruins of Varuz were plain to see and the bright morning sun only served to make their destitution all the more poignant and sorrowful. The land was empty and eerily silent. But, beside me, the Doctor was whispering these words:

'Far-called, our navies melt away;
On dune and headland sinks the fire:
Lo, all our pomp of yesterday
Is one with Nineveh and Tyre!'

*

'Another task,' said Mikhail, slowly, as if trying to guess what Conrad could have in mind. 'What might that be?'

'This Quest,' said Conrad. 'If I understand correctly what you have told me, then Aurelian is sending out his knights throughout Varuz to hunt for the Grail, whatever it might be.'

'Yes, I believe that to be true, sir,' Mikhail replied. 'And I can aid you in your own search for it. I know the lands as well as any farmer or goatherd. I have travelled them as much as any knight of Varuz. There are many dangerous corners, these days. I can guide your people through.'

'And all of this may well prove useful for your task,' Conrad said. 'But the Grail – I spoke the truth when I said I cared nothing for such a thing. So I think that we will let Aurelian's men ride wherever they wish. Let them chase whatever they like. They can go hunting for all I care. What matters to me is that while they are busy on this chase, the city lies open. Therefore we ride for the city.' He smiled at Mikhail. 'And you shall ride with us! You know the lands well, you say – and I daresay you know the city's defences well, too. This is the service that I require of you – that you bring me and my men to the gates. While Aurelian's knights are busy – we take the city. We take Varuz.'

There was a brief silence. 'Mikhail,' Clara said, in a warning voice. 'You need to be very careful now.'

'You ask a great deal of me, sir,' Mikhail said, slowly. 'To be the one that delivers Varuz into your hands?'

'Service to me requires more than the idle hunt of an idle nobility,' said Conrad fiercely. 'A chase? A quest? A grail or some other trinket? Useless!' He went over to his maps. 'I want the city. I want *Varuz*, the land between the mountains and the sea.'

'You can't ask him to do this!' Clara said. 'This is his home!'

'But I offer a great deal in return.' Conrad turned to Clara. 'You dislike me, I think, but perhaps you would like me better if you knew that I am no duke. No royal blood gave me rule. I rule through debate, persuasion, argument – aye,' he said, 'and some skill at arms. For years I have guarded our border with Varuz, preventing the crossing of those who would attack our people in their homes. Under my rule the whole world has been kept safe from the schemes and sorceries that blighted the lives of our ancestors. Never again will Varuz command our lives.' He turned back to Mikhail. 'In the old stories, I would perhaps name you my heir and put you on some throne. This I cannot do. I do not sit upon a throne. I may rule, but I cannot promise you that rule, because it is not mine to give. It was granted to me, on condition that I guarded the lands and kept the people safe. But if you achieve this task with me – you will be welcome in my country, and you will be welcome at my side. Your country, and my country – united, and the chance to prove yourself worthy in turn of the rule of it all.'

'Peace in our time,' Clara muttered to herself. To Mikhail, she said, 'Are you really falling for this? Listen to him, Mikhail! He hates Varuz. Your home. Your people. What's he offering you in return, really? A chance to stand for Parliament? And what do you think his promises are worth?' said Clara. 'He'll get you to do his dirty work, invade and conquer, and then he'll thank you by killing you.'

'Clara, please,' said Mikhail, the struggle plain on his face. 'This is not the time or the place—'

But Conrad was laughing. He reached down to his belt and drew his dagger. Then he nicked his thumb with the blade, so that a bead of blood appeared there. 'I am no great lord,' he said. 'I am no duke, with a thousand years of lineage behind me. The people of my country were asked who should rule them, and they called my name. No, I am not royal. And neither am I a liar.' He let the blood drip onto the ground. 'You have sworn an oath to serve me, Mikhail. There are witnesses here to hear me say that if that service is rendered then you will have my blessing as my successor, and the chance to prove yourself to all the people of our united countries. The chance to let them see your actions and your worth, and have them call your name – when the time comes.' The blood speckled the ground and, with the toe of his boot, Conrad rubbed it into the earth. 'My blood,' he said, 'your land. Let them be united.'

Mikhail nodded. 'Yes,' he said. 'I agree.' He looked round at the generals. 'On your honour, my lords and ladies. You have seen all this.'

Clara shook her head. 'You're making a mistake,' she said. 'A really big and really stupid mistake.'

Mikhail smiled. 'Wait and see.'

Emfil said, 'I think it's called choosing the best odds, Clara.'

'Yeah? Well, I guess we really will have to wait and see,' she said.

But the choice had been made and the deed was done. Conrad began to issue his orders. 'Send messages back over the border. Tell the companies to march for the mountains and enter Varuz.'

Mikhail started. 'This is not the whole of your force?'

'This?' Conrad smiled. 'This is only the vanguard.' He turned to Clara. 'Aurelian does not lie. Guena does not lie. And nor do I, lady. When the battle is won, you will see that Conrad, for all his roughness, is as honourable a man as all the lords and ladies of Varuz.'

Chapter

9

In time, we came to the place where the river and the road diverged, and the ruin of the bridge prevented our journey from continuing southwards. Northwards, then, we travelled, on what was left of the road, into a rough wild country. The road was soon useless, and, with its broken stones and muddy potholes, soon became a barrier in itself and a trial to the horses. We rode to the side of it and, at last, abandoned it entirely, taking to the scrubland of the northern wastes.

Here, the passing of Varuz was clearly written on the land. Now and then, we saw some fragment of its former glory: an old villa, hidden behind a line of trees; the tumbling walls of what had been a thriving village; lines of apple trees that marked where an orchard had once been. But the villas were mouldering, their roofs gone and their halls open to the rain; the villages were empty and the fields they had once served untilled; the orchards overgrown and choked with weeds and ivy. The further we went, the more barren the land became. In some places it was blackened and scorched, as if some terrible and sorcerous fire had burned it, so that grass or any good thing could no longer grow there.

I saw the Doctor's dismay on his face as we rode. Turning to me, he said, 'How long has it been like this?'

'All my life,' I said, 'and throughout my father's life, too. Each year it becomes worse, too, almost as if the land sickens. Around the city we have been protected, so far, but it will come to us too, in the end.'

'The people,' said the Doctor. 'Where are they?'

'Gone,' I said. 'Long gone.'

'Dead?'

'Not all, although there has been hunger. Some took the mountain passes, and tried for Conrad's country. But, even if they do cross over, there is not always a welcome for them there, and their lives are hard. Others left by sea, in little boats, and who knows where they have washed up? The Eastern Sea is vast. There might be lands beyond, or else perhaps one comes round the whole green world to land upon a shore only to discover that Conrad rules there. He believes he rules all the world – or nearly all the world.' I shook my head. 'I do not know the answer to this question, only that for some the risk of those open seas was better than to remain here, in Varuz. And now the exile has begun from the city. More leave, every year, and the houses stand empty.'

Throughout my speech, he had been sitting holding his metal device aloft. 'There must be a reason,' he said. 'Something must be causing this…' But if he had an answer, he did not tell me.

On we journeyed, and the Grail proved elusive. Sometimes, even this far out, we met a traveller, or even someone who had refused to leave their home, but struggled on, forcing a living from the bare land. From these people, we heard a glimmer of a tale, but each one turned out to be a false lead or a dead end. What we found were empty chapels, vain citadels, and a sad depleted land. Such failure, I thought, would surely come with a cost upon morale. I knew the men who had come with me from the city very well, having served alongside them in many border skirmishes against Conrad's incursions, and as our quest meandered on, fruitlessly, I expected to hear from them complaints about our journey and the vagueness of its purpose. I listened to their conversation, as a good captain must, but to my surprise I heard nothing but admiration for Lancelot. More than that, each one of them had a story, it seemed, about how Lancelot had spoken to him, or looked his way, or had, by some small means, conveyed his appreciation. They told these tales again and again to each other, not in competition, but it wonder, as if they must repeat how Lancelot had acknowledged them. It was strange to hear them speak, like schoolboys in awe of a respected master.

As for Lancelot's own men... a grimmer company it would be hard to imagine. Amongst my own people, as we rode, a song might every so often begin and carry us forward for a few more miles. These occasions lessened as time wore on, but from Lancelot and his knights, from the very beginning, there was nothing: no speech, no enthusiasm, and certainly no joy. They were silent, their eyes always looking forwards as if they barely saw the land through which we were passing, and it seemed to me that they begrudged every minute that we spent at rest or sleep, and would rather have ridden on, and on, beyond exhaustion. They seemed inhuman to me, like the tales of mechanical men that had come down to us from the past.

In our third week out from the city, we rode into a distant lonely country, which I had never seen before and did not know. Reaching a narrow cleft between high walls of rock, we rode through in single file, coming out into a deep valley in which lay a great lake, black and wild. On the far side, we saw an old hall, barely more than a ruin, its walls green and overgrown, and, following Lancelot's instruction, we rode round to explore.

The place, when we drew closer, had plainly been long abandoned. The roof was in tatters; the walls were barely standing. Whichever lord had lived here had departed, and the people over whom he had ruled were long gone too. Only the birds made their homes here now, and the quiet soft-footed creatures of the woods and the wild. There would be no news here of the Grail, unless carried to us upon the wind.

Here, in the poor shelter of these tumbledown walls, we made our camp. Lancelot's knights, as ever, took themselves away, and I prepared myself for sleep, but the Doctor, ever curious, wished to explore more of the hall, and at his request I went with him. And in a damp, green room without a roof, where the hangings and tapestries had been replaced by moss and ivy, we found the knight.

He was not a stranger, but one of Lancelot's

men. I wondered what had brought him away from his company, for they were closely knit and tended not to be found far from each other. Even more strangely, this one had removed his helmet and gloves – we rarely saw their faces – and his long hair, grey and wild, straggled down his back. He was standing beside the shell of a high arched window and, high above his head he was holding aloft some kind of little box. What it was I could not quite see, but lights flashed from it, and strange sounds emerged. The Doctor, however, seemed to recognise what it was, and the sight certainly surprised him.

'Oh,' he said. 'I have to say that I wasn't expecting that. I suppose I'd assumed that you would be, well, *mediaeval*.'

The knight turned to us, but only for a moment, before turning back to whatever task that he was performing.

'Doctor,' I said, 'explain this to me.'

'Our friend here,' said the Doctor, 'is using some pretty advanced tracking technology. Not as advanced as some I've seen, but advanced enough that I'd be happy to use it myself.' He moved towards the knight. 'Knights, and horses, and riding on Grail quests – it's all a performance, isn't it? What are you all about, really?'

The man did not reply, and the Doctor tapped him on the arm.

'I said, what are you all about?'

He turned to look at us properly then, and I wished that he had not for, looking into his eyes, I was filled with great grief. This man, it seemed to me, was very old, and very weary.

'Where are you from?' said the Doctor. 'Come on, tell me!'

'Doctor,' I said. 'Be gentle.'

'I don't remember,' said the knight. His voice rasped, as if rusty from disuse.

'Come on, man! Your name, at least. What's your name?'

'Doctor,' I said softly, for it seemed to me that we were tormenting a man who was already in a great deal of pain.

'I do not remember my name,' said the knight. He did not sound sorrowful, or regretful, or anything at all. He was merely stating a fact. That seemed terrible to me.

'You can't remember your *name*?' said the Doctor. 'Do you remember *anything* about yourself? Where you come from? Where you're heading?'

'The Quest,' said the knight, quickly, as if glad to be able to answer a question at last. 'I am on the Quest.'

'Yes, yes, for the Grail,' said the Doctor. 'Except that we both know that's not true.'

And indeed the old knight was shaking his head. 'Not the Grail,' he said, slowly, as if some memory was returning to him. 'No, not that. Something older than that, and much more precious. The greatest treasure in the universe – and the most deadly.'

'I see,' said the Doctor. 'Of course. I've been a fool. Not the Grail. The Glamour.'

I did not know what he meant. But his tone of voice filled me with fear.

Since the Quest had left, a great quiet had fallen upon the city, and a strange calm, as if the people had surrendered themselves to some purpose that they did not understand, and now were waiting to see if their gamble would be successful. The city-folk kept to their homes, on the whole, and, when they did come out, they gathered on corners in small groups of threes or fours to trade what information they had, and then hurried home and locked their doors.

No news came from the Quest and, after a while, it seemed to people that all that had happened was no more than a dream: that Lancelot and his company had been something they had all imagined together. But their own knights were gone – that could not be denied – and the city felt empty and unguarded without them.

At last, late one afternoon when the sun was sinking slowly into the sea, a messenger was seen heading up the road towards the city. He had plainly ridden in haste, but he did not stop to rest, and went straight to the palace and to the Great Hall, where the Duke and Duchess of Varuz sat and listened to his news. Conrad's army had been seen, far to the south, but within the borders of Varuz.

'So much for his embassy,' said Aurelian to his wife. 'His plan was always to invade, whatever message we might have sent in return. Do you see now that it was pointless to try to speak to him?'

'Maybe,' said Guena. 'But I am not the one who, believing that invasion was imminent and unavoidable, sent away the knights on a foolish errand. Aurelian, I must ask you – do you really believe that this Grail exists? That it can be found?'

Aurelian reached out to take his wife's hand. 'What else could I do? Bernhardt carries the hearts of my knights with him – and Bernhardt is loyal to you. Whatever you may think, Guena, I am no fool. Whether this Grail exists or not, I do not know. But the search for it may bring us together again.'

'Or in its failure divide us once and for all.'

'Aye,' said Aurelian, 'that might happen too.'

Guena studied him thoughtfully. 'Forgive me, Aurelian, but you seem very different from when you called upon your lords to take on this quest.'

'How so?' he said.

'You seem less enamoured of Lancelot, for one thing.'

'I will admit that when he spoke, his words swayed my heart,' Aurelian said. 'With him gone… I doubt myself.' He gave a sad smile. 'As I have always doubted myself.'

Guena squeezed his hand. 'Do not let doubt assail you any longer,' she said. 'The end is coming. Recall the knights – recall Bernhardt. Bring them back for the defence of the city.'

Aurelian shook his head. 'How can I do that?' he said. 'Who knows where the Quest has taken them? I have had no reports of them at all. All that I know is that Conrad marches for the city. We would recall Bernhardt only to have him arrive and find a city in ruins—'

'I can speak to him,' said Guena.

Aurelian looked at her in surprise. 'What do you mean?'

'The secrets of my ancestors are not all lost, Aurelian,' she said. 'I have the means to speak to Bernhardt at great range, whenever I desire.'

Aurelian sat in silence for a while, considering this news.

'You live in a city lit by means that you cannot explain, where the knights and guards carry swords that can cut through rock,' said Guena. 'Did you not think that other devices of other kinds might yet exist, left to us from my ancestors, out of happier, stronger times?'

Aurelian shifted in his seat. 'And these devices work? Have you *used* them?'

'Many times. There are people of ours in Conrad's country – people who are sympathetic to Varuz. I have spoken to them often, and given them instructions. They have struck blows on our behalf now and again, struck against Conrad's cities. From them I hear more news about Conrad's intentions than he might like.'

'What else exists?' Aurelian said, urgently. 'Are there weapons?'

'Not that I know of. Many secrets have been lost.'

There was a long pause. 'You should have told me about this,' Aurelian said. 'I am the *Duke*—'

'In name, yes. But you do not have royal blood—'

Aurelian gave a bitter laugh. 'I know, I know. Mikhail—'

'*Mikhail?*' Now it was Guena's turn to laugh bitterly. 'No,' she said, 'you never truly understood. You can rest assured that I have done all that I can for Varuz – and I shall continue to do so for as long as I am able. But time is running out. Conrad is coming, at last, and he carries with him the anger of centuries. Our forefathers were not kindly masters—'

'And I would guess that your secret assaults within his cities have not helped soften his heart towards us,' Aurelian said.

'Or perhaps they have kept him away longer, for fear of what else we might use against him,' Guena said. 'But whatever he has believed thus far, it is clear that something has happened to make him believe that he can now defeat us. He is coming. We are defenceless. We must recall the knights, and we must recall them now.' She stood, in a rustle of silk and jewels. 'I shall speak to Bernhardt and tell him to return.'

Aurelian stood. Proudly, he said, 'I would prefer that you did not speak to Bernhardt—'

'Bernhardt is the only one who can persuade those men to return,' said Guena. 'And I am the only one who can persuade him to ask. What is your preference, Aurelian? To sit and wait until Conrad arrives? Or to swallow your pride, and let me call Bernhardt home?'

They stood facing each other, face-to-face, Duke and Duchess, in opposition.

'What shall we do, Aurelian?' Guena said. 'Shall we stand here until Conrad comes, and the city burns around us? What use will our pride be to us then?' She saw him falter, and she went on in a gentler tone of voice. 'This is not the country that either of us wished to rule. How much better for us both if we could have ruled in glory over a Varuz as great as it was in its greatest days! But we were not born to those times, and we have harder, heavier choices. Perhaps the best that we can hope is that we face our end bravely. But we must not let pride stand in our way. We must call home the knights. The end is coming, and we must save whatever we can.'

'Guena,' Aurelian said, and he reached out to hold his wife's hand in his. 'You know, don't you, that I did not marry you to become Duke? That if you had been cast out of Varuz, in exile, on the road, without a chance of ever returning home, I would have loved you still. For your courage, Guena, I love you and I have always loved you.' He smiled. 'Bernhardt is wise to love you, Guena, and I know he will do whatever you ask. You love Varuz, and you are Varuz. So let us do as you wish. And when the end comes, I hope that we will all – all three of us – find peace.'

*

And it was not only the Doctor's voice that alarmed me, but the sight of that knight, so old, so weary, filled me with foreboding. 'Doctor,' I said, 'I do not understand this. We were chasing the Grail. But now you speak of "the Glamour"? What is this? What does it mean?'

'The Glamour is another myth, another legend.'

'But is this legend is true?'

'Sadly,' said the Doctor, 'it is, yes.' He looked at the knight, who had put away his little box and, as if some great weariness had overcome his limbs, was now sitting on the stone windowsill, his head bowed and his hands clasped before him.

'So what is it?' I said. 'Is it something that we should fear?'

'A wise man fears the Glamour,' said the Doctor, 'and he turns away from the chase for it. An object so powerful, so entrancing that people will kill in order to have it.'

I shuddered. 'Then it seems to me that we should follow your advice and keep well away. How will we know it when we see it? What must we watch for?'

The Doctor frowned. 'There's the difficult part, Bernhardt – the Glamour is not easy to spot. Part of its power comes from the fact that it changes depending on who is looking. And it takes on the form of their heart's desire. For one person, this might be gold, or jewels, or a painting, or a statue. For another kind of person, it might be completely different.' He looked at me slyly. 'It might, for example, appear to you as the love of your life.'

'Or as a mystery, perhaps,' I suggested, 'demanding to be solved?'

The Doctor gave me a half-smile. 'Perhaps.' He looked back at the knight. 'Or it could be a holy relic, an object of great sanctity. A Grail.'

'If it changes its appearance to suit the eye of the beholder, how then can it be found?' I pressed. 'How can one even know if one possesses it?'

The Doctor shook his head. 'You don't know. You can't know. Except when the Glamour moves on. Because then, if you're lucky, you're half the person you once were.'

'And if you are unlucky?'

'Then you're dead. Your life has drained away from you. The Glamour has taken all it can, and then it has moved on, looking for a new owner to consume.'

As the Doctor spoke, the knight shifted in his seat. A light flickered behind his eyes, some stirring of memory from a past life, perhaps. 'Aye,' he said, in a harsh voice that sounded like it came from a man dying from thirst, 'the search is endless. We have sought the Glamour for years uncounted. At first we rode from town to town on horseback, chasing stories, chasing rumours… The journeys became longer. We took to ships, and then to starships. We travelled faster than light. But always the Glamour was ahead of us. Every so often we thought we caught a glimpse of it – and even as we reached out to touch it, it was gone.'

The Doctor knelt before the knight. 'What is your name, old father?' he said, very gently. 'Can you remember your name?'

The knight tilted his head upwards, as if chasing some memory. 'My name…'

'Try,' the Doctor urged. 'Try to remember. I think it will help, if you can.'

For a moment, the knight seemed on the verge of some recollection, but then he shook his head. 'I did have a name once,' he said, 'and then another, and another, and another. All gone, long gone. What does a name matter? What does anything matter? There is only the Quest.'

The Doctor placed his hand upon the knight's. 'A cruel fate, old father,' he said.

'But could you not give up the Quest?' I said. 'Could you not stop, and rest?'

'Rest?' The knight looked at him in confusion. 'Rest?' The idea seemed to frighten him. 'We cannot rest! The Glamour! The *Glamour!*'

The Doctor pressed the man's hands between his own. 'Quiet, now,' he said. 'There's no need to become distressed.' And he talked in this way for some time, until the knight's agitation was soothed and, at last, he leaned his head back against the wall, and he slept.

A great fear had filled my heart, and a great horror too, at the sight of this old man, so old and so lost, consumed by such a terrible need that could not be satisfied. 'Doctor,' I said. 'What is this quest that we have taken on? This Glamour, this Grail – will it devour us too? Is this –' I gestured at the withered old man before us – 'is this what will happen to us? I do not wish to be one of these ghost-men, these weary creatures who are barely alive.'

Releasing the knight's hands, the Doctor stood up. 'I don't blame you, Bernhardt.' He gave me a sharp look, like a captain does when judging what strength a man has left in him. 'But I believe you at least may be impervious – or more than most. Still, perhaps we should start to consider whether you and your men might be better off leaving this quest behind and returning home—'

Even as he was speaking, I began to feel the skin around my throat become warm. I reached up my hand to touch a dark, bejewelled brooch that was fastened there. The Doctor caught the movement, and gave me a questioning look.

'It is my lady,' I said. 'She wishes to speak to me.'

The Doctor stared at the brooch at my throat. 'Oh,' he said. 'I see. I didn't realise you could get them to work at range.' Then he laughed. 'I wonder what other technology there is hiding in plain sight around here.'

Chapter

10

'What happens now?' asked the Doctor. 'How do you communicate with Guena?'

'I need to find a flat surface,' I said. 'A mirror, or plain white wall.' I looked around this broken-down hall, with weeds growing in through the window, and thick moss upon the stones. 'Where I might find something like that in such a place as this, I do not know.'

The Doctor crossed the hall to another empty shell where once a window had been. 'How about that?' he said, pointing outside.

I went to look. The window gave a view of the dark still waters of the lake. 'That,' I said, 'would work very well.'

We left the knight to his slumber, which I think was well deserved, and walked down to the shores of the lake. Its surface was preternaturally still, but this served my purpose well. I touched my fingertips to the brooch at my throat and there, in the dark water, I saw my lady's face, so dear to me, so lovely and beloved. 'Guena,' I whispered and then, out loud, I said, 'My lady Duchess. I did not think that we would have the chance to speak again.'

'Bernhardt,' she said. 'Beloved.'

Against all reason, we both reached out then, our fingertips rippling the water and the images of each other in a futile but mutual attempt to touch. When the water settled again, she was there once more, as clear as day. 'Come back,' she said to me. 'Please, Bernhardt, come back.'

I shook my head. 'I cannot do that, my lady. I made a promise to the Duke to ride with this company until the Grail was found.'

'Aurelian and I have spoken,' she said. 'We have made a kind of peace. And I have other news. Conrad has brought a great army across the mountains. He is coming. We need you to come back, and we need you to bring our knights back with you.'

I almost laughed out of bitterness. 'Return? You want me to return? How shall I do that, lady? You ask me to bring the knights with me? But you do not know what you ask. The knights are lost

to me, Guena. I have no power over them. Bring
them back? How should I do this? They will hear
no appeal that I can give. They hear only Lancelot
now.'

She looked back at me in confusion and alarm.

'And even if we should return, each one of us
that was sent off on this fruitless, benighted quest,
what hope is there?' I said. 'Conrad's army comes,
you say, and I guess that it will be greater than any
force we can marshal against him. What purpose
would be served by our return, except for us all to
die together?'

'Bernhardt,' she said, and I could see that she
was grieved. Never had I spoken so freely with
her before, and certainly never so angrily. 'You are
much changed—'

'A man does not take to banishment easily,' I
replied. 'It seems that it comes with a cost.'

Behind me, the Doctor cleared his throat,
making his presence clear to Guena for the first
time. 'Should I, er, go? Leave you to it? Whatever
it is? This sounds like it's getting very, um, well…'

'Holy man,' my lady said. She looked away
from me to address the Doctor. 'You seem always
to be on hand to help, or, at least to hear what is
happening. No, no, do not go! Indeed, perhaps you
can help me now? For it seems to me that Lord

Bernhardt has lost his way in the time that he has been away from me.'

'Yes, I've been thinking much the same thing. But you, know, Duchess, this wild country out here is a hard sight for a man who loves his land as much as Bernhardt.' The Doctor eyed me thoughtfully. 'Still,' he said to me, 'I thought you were a wiser man than this. Have you forgotten everything we've seen today?' I shivered at the thought of that ghost-man, the Glamour Knight, sleeping now against the window in that green chamber behind us. 'Don't you see, Bernhardt? That's what the Glamour does to people. It drains them dry until nothing remains of what they were. It changes them beyond recognition. But it's different, depending on the person. It can find other weaknesses to exploit. So don't let your pride, or your anger, or your despair – whatever it is – do the same to you, Bernhardt. Let it go from you. Or you might not stay the man you are.'

I heard his words, and I understood their meaning, but still I hesitated.

'Have you really gone so far from yourself in such a short time, Bernhardt?' the Doctor said. 'The man I met only a short time ago would have dropped everything to ride to aid his city at his lady's request. Has this quest made you lose so much of yourself, so quickly?'

I felt at war with myself then. A part of me wished dearly to return to my city, of course, and to see my lady again. But a part of me could not see what purpose would be served, other than to hasten my death. Perhaps this quest would be better than any return; perhaps it would be better to lose myself in chasing a dream, a beautiful, impossible dream…

'I shall speak to the knights,' I said, with some effort, but even as I spoke it felt as if a great weight was lifting from me, and as I continued, I felt lighter than I had in years. 'But I can make no promises, Guena. You have not seen the changes that have overcome them. Some are nothing like the men that I have known for years. They are enamoured of this Lancelot, and under his sway. But I shall do whatever I can, and the best that I can. For you.'

The Doctor slapped me on the back. 'Good man!'

'Thank you, Bernhardt,' said my lady. 'And you too, Doctor. Now – it is possible that I might be able to perform a small service for you. Your companion – Clara – have you had word from her?'

'No,' said the Doctor, in a worried voice. 'Nothing at all.'

'Then perhaps I may try to reach her. We can speak to her together.'

The Doctor looked at her hopefully. 'You can do that?'

'I can make no promises,' said my lady. 'Before, if I have communicated with someone at a great distance, I have always known where they are. I do not, of course, know exactly where Clara is. But I can see no harm in trying.'

'You reached Bernhardt,' the Doctor said. 'You didn't know where we were.'

She smiled. 'Between Bernhardt and myself, there is never any real distance. Let us hope that I can reach Clara too, even if I do not know her well.'

The Doctor nodded his agreement. 'Whatever you can do, Duchess, I'd be grateful.'

My lady closed her eyes.

'She will do it, Doctor,' I said. 'She is without compare.'

On Mikhail's advice, Conrad's army had come down the mountains by a different way from the one that he, Clara and Emfil had taken upwards. Although the route was longer, the paths were wider and coped more readily with the men and horses and equipment that the army brought with them. They came into Varuz well south of the river, after which they followed the old road north. The land in this country was flat and to

Clara's eyes it looked as if, in better days, it would have been fertile and well farmed. But the villages were empty, the doors of the cottages barred, and the fields and barns had been abandoned. Some had clearly been deserted for many years but, as they drew nearer to the river, it was clear that news of the oncoming army had passed this way, and the people had only recently fled. To the city, Clara guessed, since she had gathered from what was being said that the lands north of the river were wild and inhospitable, and they had seen no refugees on the road. But fleeing to the city was only delaying the inevitable, Clara thought, sadly. Conrad's army was implacable.

The march north took them over a week and, when they reached the banks of the river, Clara thought that surely there would now be a further significant delay. But the river posed no problem to Conrad's men and, with the air of a task that had been much executed, they brought out bridging equipment. They moved with terrifying speed, and it was only a matter of hours before Conrad was able to cross the river and lead his army onto the road that led towards the city of Varuz.

In all this time, Clara had had little chance to speak to Mikhail. As befitted his new status as the newest of the generals – and the one who had the most local knowledge – he was riding in the vanguard with Conrad. She and Emfil, meanwhile, had been kept at the centre of the company, under watchful eyes.

Dusk approached, and they made camp. Emfil took the chance to stretch his legs, but Clara, exhausted from the day's travelling, decided to get straight to sleep. She filled a basin of water to wash. Looking down, she saw the face of the Doctor in front of her.

'Oh, come off it,' she told herself. 'You're not that tired.'

She rubbed her eyes. But there he was still, eyebrows on the march, gurning and gesticulating and looking ludicrous.

'This,' said Clara, 'is not fair.' She waved her hands to shoo the hallucination. 'Go away! I'm tired! I want to go to sleep!'

It didn't work. The Doctor only looked even more annoyed. This was what persuaded her that it probably wasn't a dream but was actually him.

'All right,' she said, as he waved his hands and pointed. 'I'm listening. What do you want me to do?'

It took a while, but eventually Clara realised that he was pointing to her neck, where the pendant lay. She pulled it out and held it between her hands.

The Doctor gestured that she should rub it, so she did. Soon enough she could hear his voice. '… not sure how I can make this any clearer, Clara!'

Sound on.

'Oh, *that's* what this is for,' Clara said. 'Hi, Doctor. I can hear you now.'

Communications established, the first thing the Doctor did, inevitably, was to start to complain. 'Where have you got to? It's *hopeless* without you. People keep thinking I'm being rude! I don't know what you do to stop them getting angry with me.'

'I imagine that they're angry because you *are* being rude,' said Clara. 'As to where I've been – I got banished. Remember that bit? I got marched out of the city under pain of death, by people waving laser-swords around! And then I walked halfway up a mountain and got captured by Conrad and now I'm halfway back to the city again, stuck in the middle of a massive army set on taking the city—'

The Doctor waved his hand in dismissal. 'Oh, that's nothing. You won't believe what's been happening here.'

'Do you mean the bit where a knight called Lancelot turned up looking for the Holy Grail?' She heard quiet laughter in the background. 'Is that you, Lord Bernhardt?'

Bernhardt's thin face came into view. 'Lady

Clara,' he said, with a smile. 'You lighten the heart, as ever.'

'How did you know that?' the Doctor said furiously.

'Mikhail turned up,' Clara said. 'He told me all about what was happening.'

The Duchess of Varuz spoke. 'Mikhail?' She sounded startled. 'Is he there?'

'Wow,' said Clara. 'The gang's all here. Yes, I met Mikhail in the mountains. He seemed to know a lot more about what was going on than I thought was possible, given he'd been given his marching orders with us. I suppose you've been telling him, Guena.'

'We may have had some contact, yes.'

'Well, he's here all right, but if you're hoping he'll persuade Conrad to see the error of his ways, forget it. He's riding up at the front of the army. Conrad's like a long-lost dad. I wouldn't rely on any help from Mikhail.'

'I see,' said Guena. She was palpably grieved. 'But how can I blame him?'

'You made some *really* bad decisions there,' Clara said.

'We were trying to protect him,' Guena said.

'Well, it hasn't worked,' said Clara. 'And now it's payback.'

'If Mikhail has turned against us, we are worse

now than undefended,' Bernhardt said. 'Someone who knows the land and the city well, telling Conrad all he knows.' A note of despair was creeping into his voice. 'And I do not believe many of the knights will give up this quest. Not while Lancelot holds such power over them…'

'Doctor,' said Clara, 'is this whole thing about the Grail true? Is it really Lancelot? That would be *amazing!*'

'No, of course it's not true!' the Doctor said. 'Can we get one thing absolutely straight? The Grail is a story, a myth! It didn't exist on your world! It can't exist here!'

Clara pressed on. 'But this Lancelot, whoever he is – he believes that it exists. Bernhardt, you say that the knights won't come back without Lancelot commanding them to return. Is that right?'

'I fear so, Clara.'

'But Lancelot won't return to the city unless he thinks the Grail is there…'

'Where are you going with this, Clara?' said the Doctor.

'Well, there's someone here who might be able to help, but he might need some persuading.' She looked down at the pendant. 'Guena, are you the only one who can start conversations? Or can I use this to communicate back?'

'Yes,' said the Duchess, 'The device is configured now to respond to the rest of us. You will need a clear surface – a mirror, or a basin of water. Take the jewel and warm it. I will know that you wish to speak to me; so will Bernhardt, and through him you can speak to the Doctor.'

'Mirror, water – something clear; warm the jewel; got all that. All right,' Clara said. 'I'm going offline now and I'm going to try something that's probably quite stupid.'

'Clara,' said the Doctor. 'What are you doing?'

'Don't worry,' said Clara. 'I'm sure everything will turn out just fine.'

She left the tent, and went in search of Emfil. She found him wandering near the edge of the camp, looking past the guards intently. She crept up behind him and tapped him on the shoulder. He jumped.

'Hello,' she said. 'Are you planning on skipping out on me again?'

He gave her a guilty look. 'Clara, this has all got too much for me. I'm not an adventurer, you know. I'm just—'

'Yes, yes, a collector.'

'I'm only trying to find the Glamour.'

'Well,' said Clara, 'as luck would have it, I think that our paths are leading us the same way. If you're looking for the Glamour that means you're looking for Lancelot. And so am I, now. So let's go together. Again.'

'Why should I take you with me?' said Emfil.

'Because I know exactly where he is.'

Emfil looked at her suspiciously. 'And why do you want to take me with you?'

'Because I need a favour.' Clara grinned. 'What do you say? One more adventure?'

He looked at her doubtfully. 'If we must.'

'Good,' said Clara. 'Now, I know you're not much of a jewel thief, but how are you when it comes to horse rustling?'

We came, the Doctor and I, to Lord Lancelot's tent, at the centre of our encampment. We were surprised to find it unguarded, but perhaps that old knight no longer cared for the perils of the world. We slipped inside easily, and found the space within so dark that at first I believed that Lancelot was not there. Surely nobody could spend the hours in such a gloom? But as my eyes became accustomed to the darkness, I made out a chair at the far side of the tent, and, sitting upon it, Lancelot himself. His head slumped down, chin almost to his chest, and I would have thought he was asleep, except that as we approached I caught a glimmer of his eyes beneath his lashes. Did he sit here often in the dark, I wondered, brooding over the long years of his quest, and the absence of the treasure which he sought?

'My lord,' I said, to him. 'I have important news. I received a summons from the Duke, asking me to return speedily to the defence of our city. Therefore I beg leave to depart from your company at once, and to return home.'

The knight did not lift his head.

'My lord,' I said. 'I do not know how much you learned of us during your short visit, or what you have gleaned from us upon our journey together. But a great army approaches our city, and it is set upon our destruction. We must return home, the knights and I. We must join the defence of our home.'

He still gave no reply, and I was beginning to doubt whether he was well. Slowly, I stepped forwards, and this movement roused him at last from his stupor. 'Sir,' I said. 'May I have your leave to return home? Will you release me, and those who came with me?'

He looked at me then through eyes that I think had seen more than I will ever dream or understand. How long had this man been travelling? How weary must he have been?

'Only your own will holds you here,' he said. 'I cannot force you to stay, nor could I stop you from leaving.'

'And the rest of the knights?' said the Doctor. 'Will you keep them here?'

'Ask them,' said Lancelot. 'They can speak for themselves.'

'And you, sir,' I said, thinking that while I had the chance I would make my appeal to him. 'Will you come back with us, with your company? The Duke made you welcome in his hall, sir. He sent men with you that he could ill afford to lose. Soon our city will be in desperate straits. Will you come with me, sir, to our aid?'

Lancelot's head fell back against his chest. 'The Quest is all that matters,' he said. 'We cannot abandon the Quest.'

I tried a few more times, but he would not speak again, and at length, the Doctor signalled to me that we should leave. 'Well,' he said, when we came out into the cool, welcome air, 'you've got your answer. You can go whenever you like and take whoever wants to go back with you. The question now is whether you can *find* anyone who wants to go back with you.'

And so it proved. One by one, I spoke to the men who had set out with me that morning from the city, a hundred of them all told, and for each one who said that he would return with me, another four said that they would not forsake the Quest for the Grail. Even when I told them of the approach of Conrad's army, they could not be persuaded. But I could not judge them cowards or deserters. It was plain to me that whatever love they had had for Aurelian had been replaced now with reverence for that ancient and weary knight whose presence I had just left. A great power Lancelot held over them, and they would not now be torn from him.

'I'll keep trying,' the Doctor said to me. 'After you're gone, I'll keep on at them. I'll try to send more after you.'

This news was bad. 'Doctor,' I said, 'do I understand you correctly? Do you not ride with me for my home?'

He shook his head. 'I'm staying here,' he said. 'There might still be something I can do.'

'I am grieved at this news,' I said. 'I believe you would be a great help to us back at the city. But I think that I could not persuade you to depart yet.' I smiled. 'Your mystery is not yet solved, is it? Lancelot casts his own, particular spell over you.'

The Doctor looked perturbed by that suggestion. 'I don't think that's why I'm staying,' he said. 'At least, I *hope* that's not why… But, you're right, Bernhardt.

I don't like an unsolved mystery. And the presence here of a man named Lancelot – whoever he might be in reality – remains unexplained. So stay here I will, until I have a satisfactory explanation. But if I happen to use my time to persuade a few more of your recalcitrant knights that their duty is with their city and their Duke rather than here – then that's surely to the good.' He must have seen my expression, because he added, 'I'm not walking out on you, Bernhardt. I promise you, I always turn up again – usually when I'm least expected.'

And since I could hardly force him to come with me – and I did not want to force him – this was our goodbye, at least, I hoped, for the present.

In the end, a scant twenty of us set out to return to our city, barely a fifth of the proud company that had set out those weeks before. At least our journey home was the by the quickest way: we had no need stray down every lane, chasing stories; we did not stop by dark and lonely lakes in the hope that someone there remained who could give us word of the long-lost Grail. No, our purpose – our quest – was clear. To come to our city by the swiftest route, and, reaching our home, to bring what aid we could, and, more, to bring heart to the people there, in their most desperate hour. So quickly did we ride, hardly stopping to eat or to sleep, that I barely had time to think what welcome I might receive from Aurelian. But when we turned the bend in the road, and my city came into view, my heart sank in my chest, and I was afraid.

The welcome we received from the people as we rode through the city was, at least, very warm, even at the sight of so few of us. Cheers rose up as we passed through, and flowers were thrown before us, and I knew that, whatever the cost might be to myself personally, this had been the right decision.

And, in the end, our meeting was not as terrible as I had feared. When we came to the palace, the honour guard welcomed us with silver trumpets. At their sound, the Duke and the Duchess came out, hand in hand, and greeted us. And then Aurelian turned to me, and welcomed me with open arms, and we made our peace, and the three of us together took counsel, and prepared ourselves to stand alongside each other in the battle that was soon to come.

Chapter

11

The plan, Clara had to admit, was not exactly sophisticated: wait till dark, slip away from their guards, then find a couple of spare horses and make a mad dash for it. So she was surprised at how smoothly it was going. She and Emfil sneaked out of the back of their tent, and wandered through the camp, until they spotted two horses standing quietly by themselves, grazing on the grass. 'They'll do,' said Clara. 'Come on, we can't waste time.'

But as they crept towards the horses, a tall figure came out of the shadows to bar their way. 'My friends,' said Mikhail. 'I thought you might try to leave us.'

'And I there I was thinking that you'd forgotten us,' said Clara. 'What with your new fancy friends and your being a traitor and everything.'

'Lady Clara,' he said, with a smile. 'You must surely know that you are quite unforgettable. So, friends – tell me where you are going, and why?'

'That's easy,' said Emfil, frankly. 'I want to get away. I don't want to be in the middle of a war. Who wants to be in the middle of a war?'

'And you, Clara? Does battle frighten you in the same way?'

'Of course it does,' said Clara. 'I'm not daft. But that's not why I'm going, and you know it. Where do you think I'm going?'

Mikhail folded his arms. 'Not to the city, I think. You would be trapped there, and you are not the kind of person who would choose inaction over action. No, I think that you go in search of your friend the Doctor, and in search of Lancelot.' He looked over his shoulder. 'Tell me, do these horses meet your requirements?'

Clara stared at him. 'Hang on,' she said. 'Did you leave them here for us?'

'If I wanted you to remain here, Clara, you would remain here. The guards were sent away from your tent, the horses have been brought here for you to discover. You will find your path unbarred when you leave.'

'Does Conrad know about this?' she said.

Mikhail gave a crooked smile. So he wasn't

entirely at Conrad's beck and call.

'I don't understand,' Clara said. 'Why are you letting us go?'

'In the case of this one,' he nodded at Emfil. 'I see no purpose in trapping him in the middle of a battle. He is afraid, and he may prove a liability.'

Emfil nodded vigorously. 'Absolutely,' he said. 'Disastrous to keep me around. I'll only get in the way.'

'And in your case, Clara – I do not believe you would do us harm, and I would not hold you here against you will. You have embroiled yourself in our affairs, but they are not yours and, besides, you have only ever acted in the cause of peace.' He moved out of her way. 'Go where you will.'

'That's very decent of you,' she said.

'I am a better man that you think,' he replied.

Clara offered Mikhail her hand. He was confused for a moment by what this meant, and then understood, taking her hand and clasping it within her own. 'Good luck, Mikhail,' Clara said. 'I hope you know what you're doing.'

'You'll see,' he said. 'In the end, this will be for the best.'

'Not for Aurelian, I think,' Clara said.

'No,' said Mikhail, and Clara thought she heard regret there. 'Not for him.'

They took the horses and left. As Mikhail had promised, their way was clear, and soon they were far from the army and riding north, through wild and empty country. 'Look out for water,' Clara said, and, at last, abandoning their attempt to find a pool or a lake, they stopped and she knelt down beside a muddy puddle on the road.

'What *are* you doing?' said Emfil.

Clara was hunched over the puddle, blowing on the pendant and muttering under her breath. 'I'm trying to speak to the Doctor. I can't get this to work!'

'I can only speak for myself,' Emfil said, 'but I've never seen a communications device that involves crouching over a puddle and huffing.'

'Guena said this would *work*…'

'Perhaps,' Emfil said, 'you could try more traditional means?'

Clara looked up. 'What do you mean?'

'I took a look ahead. Lancelot's company is camped about half-a-mile along the road. If the Doctor's there, you can go and talk to him.'

Clara felt a rush of relief. She jumped to her feet and gave Emfil a hug, which left the explorer quite flustered. 'Come on,' she said. 'Everything will be fine if we can find the Doctor.'

They entered the camp quite easily, and passed

through it easily too. None of the knights paid them any attention; they seemed wrapped up in their tasks, or else in a dreamy state, their thoughts elsewhere. Then Clara saw a familiar face – but not Bernhardt or the Doctor. It was the grey-haired soldier she had met on her first day in Varuz; the one who had accompanied her and the Doctor to the palace, and had been such a thorn in Mikhail's side. She wondered what he would think, if he knew what Mikhail was doing now.

'Hello,' Clara said. 'Fancy seeing you here.'

The man turned to look at her. At first, his expression was a blank, and then, slowly, recognition returned. 'Lady Clara.' A cloud passed over his face. 'Weren't you meant to have left Varuz?' He shrugged. 'It does not matter, I suppose.'

Clara frowned. 'What do you mean? Has Conrad taken the city already?' Surely it was another couple of days before the army could reach the gates? The battle couldn't be over already?

'Conrad?' Again, the soldier looked bewildered. 'Ah, of course! No, I have no news of Conrad. Does he ride to Varuz?'

'Yes, he rides,' said Clara. 'He rides with a great big army behind him, and he's nearly at the city gates. Listen, where's the Doctor? Where's Bernhardt?'

But the man's attention had already strayed, and he was turning away. Clara grabbed his arm – and his lack of response to this action was what finally convinced her that something very strange was happening here.

'Hey,' she said. 'Where's Bernhardt?'

'Bernhardt? He's gone. He left us.'

'And the Doctor?'

The soldier shrugged. Clara sighed. 'So why did Bernhardt leave?'

'The Quest proved too much for him.'

'The Quest?' said Clara. 'Go on, tell me about that.'

'For the Grail.' The soldier's eyes began to shine. 'All my life,' he said, 'there was nothing of meaning. Nothing of purpose. But now...' He held out his hands and looked past them both, his face enraptured. 'I've seen it in my dreams. If only I can touch it before I die... The Grail!'

Beside Clara, Emfil was fiddling surreptitiously with one of his gadgets. 'I'm not sure it's here, Clara. The readings are baffling: half-here, half-absent. Like it was back in the city.' He frowned. 'I don't understand this...'

'Perhaps it was back in the city all along,' said Clara. 'That's where all the technology is. You're picking up some trace of that, maybe.'

Emfil nodded. 'I suppose that could be the case…' He gave a frustrated sigh. 'If it's back in the city, I was so close! It might have been within my grasp!'

'That's all right,' said Clara, 'because we're going back.'

'Back? Back where?'

'To the city.'

'Er, Clara,' Emfil looked nervous, 'wasn't there an army heading that way?'

'That's right.'

'A big army.'

'A very big army.'

'Which probably means, well, you know, a *battle*…?'

'You're on fire today, Emfil.' Clara folded her arms. 'Are you serious about getting your hands on the Glamour or not?'

Emfil gave her a sorrowful look. 'More than anything else in the universe.'

'Then we should go back to the city – but we need to bring these knights with us.' She looked around. The soldier to whom had been talking had wandered away. 'I don't think they'll leave without Lancelot, though. So I need your help.'

Emfil looked doubtful. 'Weren't you looking for the Doctor?'

'He'll be at the city. He's always where the trouble is. Are you coming? Or were you not really interested in the Glamour after all?'

With a sigh, Emfil followed Clara as they wandered through the camp in search of Lancelot. They found the captain of the company in his tent, sitting with his head down, in the dark.

'Hello?' Clara called, lifting the flap of the tent. 'Are you at home to visitors?'

Lancelot did not move or answer.

'I just want a quick word,' Clara said. 'If that's OK?'

'Is he asleep?' whispered Emfil. 'I think he's asleep.'

'He's a legend,' said Clara. 'Legends don't sleep. They're too busy being legendary. Hey, Lancelot!' said Clara. Lancelot did not reply. She had no idea whether he was listening or, indeed, whether he was even awake, but she carried on nevertheless. 'You're heading the wrong way. The Grail – it's not here. It's back at the city. My friend – Emfil – that's what he thinks, and he knows all about it.' She turned to him. 'Don't you, Emfil?'

'Er…'

'Come on!' She tugged at his arm. 'Tell the man what you know.'

Nervously, Emfil stepped forwards, holding up

his tracker. 'Um. Yes. Well. The Grail – only it's not the Grail you're really after, is it? It's the Glamour.'

Was it Clara's imagination, or did Lancelot stir at that?

'I've been tracking it too,' Emfil said. 'I tracked it to this world, same as you. And my readings – they, er, suggest that we should be back at the city. That the Glamour is back at the city.' He turned to Clara and whispered, 'Actually, that's not strictly true—'

'Shut up,' advised Clara, and then she addressed Lancelot again. 'The problem is, that there's an army on the way to the city, and the man leading it, Conrad, doesn't care about grails or glamours. He just wants to destroy the city.'

Now the old legend was definitely listening. His head was up, and he was staring at them both.

'So my advice to you, Sir Lancelot,' said Clara, 'is that you all hop on your horses and get back to the city pretty darn quick, or else soon there won't be a Glamour. The city will be ruined, and the Glamour will go with it.'

Lancelot sat for a while in silent contemplation. Then, with a swiftness of purpose that Clara would not have believed the old knight could show, he rose to his feet and strode out of the tent. Standing outside he called out his orders.

'My knights!' he cried. 'We ride! We make for the city! There we will find what we most desire!' And all the company – Glamour Knights and men of Varuz alike – jumped to obey his command.

'OK,' Clara said to herself. 'That was slightly easier than I was expecting.' Then she sighed. 'But Doctor – where *are* you?'

Two days after the first messenger arrived reporting that Conrad was on his way, more messengers arrived to tell us that the river had been crossed, and that the army was no more than a day's march from the city gates. All that day, therefore, we hurried to bring in whoever was beyond the city walls. Refugees had been arriving in a slow trickle throughout that week, and on this last day a few hardy souls from the north country arrived. They brought with them a tale of a party of grim knights who had passed their way, heading further into waste lands, on a strange quest. My heart sank, for it seemed to me that the Doctor had failed in his attempt to send more men our way. Any knight of Varuz who changed his mind now would leave Lancelot and arrive only to find a city in ruins.

That night we hoped that there were no more people to come, and the gates were closed. The next day, we awoke to see the army advancing down the road. They were a terrible sight, but, to my mind, the worst sight of all was Mikhail's banner – the blue and gold of the Duke's heir – flying beside Conrad's. I pondered again all the choices that we had made concerning this young man, and in the end decided that at least, this way, he would live, should Conrad not prove treacherous. Had he become Duke, he would have been standing here with us, facing his certain death. For we did not doubt the outcome, only what the course of events would be. All that morning we watched Conrad's men make camp, and then begin to bring out their great engines of war. We were besieged – and we knew it was only a matter of time before we were lost.

We, those knights of Varuz who had returned, gathered with the Duke and the Duchess in the Great Hall, where we considered our options. 'The sea routes are controlled by Conrad,' I said. 'The river too. The gates are closed, and whatever stores we have must last the whole of the siege.'

'Which might not be long,' said Aurelian. 'Conrad has been preparing for this for a long time. And no relief coming to us, unless Guena knows something that the rest of us do not.'

We all looked hopefully at the Duchess then, and I admit that I wondered whether indeed she had some final resources hidden away about which we knew nothing. But she shook her head. 'I only ever had a handful of people in Conrad's country. Those who have not returned are still there.'

'But the devices that you have,' urged Aurelian. 'Is there anything that might help us? Our ancestors ruled the whole world! They walked amongst the stars!'

'If my father the Duke knew anything about them, he never taught me. Perhaps he intended to show Mikhail, one day… But I was only a daughter. All that he showed me were the mirrors, the means to speak to people at great distance. There is no army coming, Aurelian, and there are no weapons hidden away, or none that I know about.'

The sun was setting. Aurelian stood in front of his throne and watched the red light upon the walls. 'I chafe at this inaction,' he said. 'And I will not sit here to starve. In the morning, I will open the gates, and I will ride out and bring battle to Conrad – and to Mikhail.' He looked around us all standing there. 'Who is with me?'

This time there was no hesitation. 'You know that I am, my lord,' I said. 'And all these men here today, they are with you, and they stand beside you until the very end.'

And his court of knights, although much

depleted, took up my words, and each one of them swore to Aurelian that he would stand beside him in this last battle. I saw Guena, sitting on her chair beside the Duke, smiling at me, and I was glad.

We were busy then through much of the night, preparing for the morning. In the last dark hours before the dawn, however, I was able to go to my rooms for a little while and I slept, dreamlessly, taking solace in the darkness and oblivion. A little before dawn, I woke, and got ready to join the others, but not before speaking to my lady one last time. But of that parting, I will say nothing here.

Dawn broke, and we took up our positions. At a sign from Aurelian, the gates opened, and we rode through. Silver trumpets sang to announce the coming of the Duke. And, from the north, there came an answer. I looked and saw what I had not believed possible: there, riding towards the city, was our relief. Lancelot had arrived, and with him came the last company of knights of Varuz. And then I saw Mikhail riding towards the Duke, and everything was lost in the blur of battle.

Clara and Emfil had not taken part in the charge. Instead, a few miles before Lancelot and his men came to the city, they had held back and then, when all the company had passed them, they rode off. Nobody paid them any attention. The Grail was their object, not two riders slipping away into the hills. When they reached a good height, near a little stream, they stopped, and sat down to watch the battle beneath them. They heard the trumpets announce the opening of the gates, and saw Aurelian, his armour gleaming in the sun, ride out to meet his enemy. They heard the trumpets sound in reply, and saw Lancelot and his company ride onto the field. They watched Lancelot identify the captain of the enemy, and make his way through the chaos to Mikhail.

They fought for what seemed like an age. The young lord had speed and agility, but the old knight had cunning and guile. Still, it was Mikhail who struck the first real blow, coming in low beneath Lancelot's defences, and slicing upwards with the bright laser of his sword. Clara gasped as Lancelot staggered and fell back.

Lancelot was wounded, and badly – but there was no blood. Instead, from the wound in his chest there poured out a great golden light, as if he was a clear glass vessel through which the sun was shining. Slowly, this light enveloped him, becoming brighter and brighter all the while, so that Clara's eyes began to water, and she had to put her hand up to shade them. For a split second, she thought she saw something forming at the heart of the light, a dark empty shape, but then, suddenly, the light burst outwards, almost blinding her. She had to look away. When she was able to see again, there was nothing there. Lancelot was gone.

The battle had ceased. Silence had descended across the field. Mikhail was standing staring around in bewilderment, looking for his enemy. His laser sword was still drawn, but the light emanating from that seemed barely anything now, like the sputtering flame of a candle that has burned low. His men stood back, uneasily, waiting for his commands.

'What just happened?' said Clara.

Beside her, Emfil was busy with his tracker. 'Oh,' he said. 'I think I understand.'

'Well, I don't,' Clara said. 'So what's going on?'

'The Glamour wasn't here at the city at all – well, not until Lancelot and his knights arrived.'

Clara frowned at him. 'What do you mean? They already had the Glamour, but they didn't realise it?'

Emfil was laughing. 'Oh, it's more than that, Clara. Don't you get it? Think about it. The knights all love him. He had them under a spell. They wanted to be close to him. They forgot about everything else when he was around. Lancelot didn't carry the Glamour with him. He *is* the Glamour!'

Clara looked down at the battlefield. 'And now he's gone…'

And his men prepared to follow. Slowly, the company of Glamour Knights, the last defence of the city, assembled themselves into their ranks. Five by six, thirty grim and weary knights, as ancient as time, whose names and stories were long gone, whose only purpose now was the quest upon which they had spent uncounted years, a quest that could never be satisfied, since, unwittingly, they already carried with them the object of their desire.

'They're going,' said Clara. 'They're leaving…'

'Chasing the Glamour,' said Emfil. 'Following Lancelot, wherever he goes.'

The knights were assembled. Each one lifted his closed fist to press it against his breast, and then a mist seemed to descend upon them, and, when it lifted, they were gone.

'Transporter,' said Emfil. 'They're back on their ship.' He stood up. 'Clara, I'm sorry.'

She turned to him. 'Emfil? Where are you going?'

'I can't lose them. I can't let them get away! Not now I know what the Glamour is.' His face was in rapture. 'Did you see it? It was so beautiful!'

'Oh, I see.' Clara reached out to take his hand. 'Emfil, don't go! Can't you see there's no point? The Glamour – you can't collect it and put it away and bring it out to look at it whenever you want. You can't own something like that. It will only own you!'

But she could see that she was wasting her breath. He was far away from her, long gone, his eyes fixed on the spot where the great golden light had first transfigured Lancelot, and then carried him away. 'So beautiful,' he said. 'I knew it would be. I just hadn't imagined *how* beautiful… It was so close, and now it's gone!' He nearly sobbed. 'But now I know what I'm looking for. Now I know…' He turned back to her, briefly. 'Goodbye, Clara! You don't know how you've helped me! I'm so grateful! Now I really think I'm going to find it! No, I *know* that I am! One last journey and I'll be there! I'll have it! The Glamour!'

He reached down to his belt, and tapped his finger against one of the gadgets there. A silver shimmer engulfed him, and then he was gone, leaving Clara standing there with her hand still stretched out, but now empty.

'I don't think I helped at all,' she said to the space where Emfil had been standing. Then she looked down at the battlefield.

The knights were gone. The city was undefended. She watched as Mikhail collected himself, and started issuing orders. Conrad's army began to pull itself back into line, and then turned towards the city gates.

Chapter

12

Guena, watching in her mirror from the palace, saw the whole day as it happened too. She saw the gate open, and Aurelian ride out. She saw Mikhail and Lancelot meet in combat, and the old knight's strange change. She saw him disappear, and his men follow, and then she saw Mikhail gather his wits, and turn to face Aurelian.

She did not need to see any more. Leaving behind her mirror, she made her way towards the secret routes through the palace. She knew she did not have long. Aurelian would be dead soon, and Mikhail would ride into the city, and, whatever her nephew might wish to do, she did not think that Conrad's men would show her mercy.

At last, Mikhail delivered the death blow, and the last Duke of Varuz died defending his city, as he had hoped that he would. Then Conrad's army passed through the gates.

The moment that I saw that light emerge from Lancelot and grasped the truth of his nature, I knew that the city was lost. I did not need to wait to see the end, because I knew now how this story would end. I knew Lancelot and his knights were leaving, and that with their departure Mikhail and Conrad would together take the city, and that poor Aurelian would make his last stand and die... And so it happened. All that remained unclear to me was whether my lady was alive, and, if so, whether I could, against hope, save her. If this makes me a coward, then so be it. But the battle was lost, and nothing I could do would prevent that. But I could still save Guena. And so I left the men of war to their affairs, and I followed my heart's desire, back into the city.

I ran through streets filled with people terrified of what the next few hours would bring, and raced towards the palace. Long ago, Guena had told me the secret routes in and out, and I took a narrow street that led to one of these. I reached a small door, and I used the key that Guena had given me, and rushed inside. I hurried down a little corridor, but soon I was stopped in my tracks.

The way was blocked. I nearly wept. A huge box, the like of which I had never seen, dark blue with strange white lettering upon it. What was this monstrosity? How had it come here? And, more to the point, how could I get past?

As I was pondering this dilemma, a door on the box opened, and I beheld a familiar face.

'Doctor!' I cried. 'I thought you were gone!'

'What?' He stepped out of the box and closed the door behind him. 'Did you think I wasn't coming back? I said I'd come back.'

'Aye, when least expected. And you were true to your word!'

He looked up and around, listening to the sounds of war from beyond the palace, as if taking the measure of the city and what was happening all round. 'Sometimes,' he said to himself, 'war just happens, however hard you try.' Then he looked at me, very sharply. 'You didn't care for the fight?'

'No,' I said.

'Good man. I imagine that you're looking for Guena in all this chaos.'

'I am, but…' I pointed at the blue box. 'There is an impediment.'

'An impediment? The TARDIS? I think of her more as an enabler. Anyway, you can't get through this way – the walls are already down.'

I felt the life drain from me. 'Then she is lost,' I said. 'Everything is lost.'

'Perhaps,' he said, looking beyond me. 'Perhaps not.'

I turned to see what had attracted his attention.

It was my lady, Guena, She had come another way.

'You just can't keep a good duchess down,' said the Doctor. He watched uncomfortably as we embraced. 'Hugging,' he said mournfully. 'There's always hugging. Always. But if you're done, I still need to get to Clara.'

Guena touched the jewel on one of her rings. 'I could speak to Clara with this,' she said. 'If she is near water, or can find something to use—'

'No!' said the Doctor quickly, putting his hand out to stop Guena. Both of us were startled at the vehemence of his response. 'No,' he said. 'Listen to me, Guena. You're not to use these things again. These devices of yours – you said you didn't know how they worked. Well, it's never good to use things that you don't really understand. Electricity, fusion, fission – oh, they're all great, but you need to know what you're doing. And you really don't know what you're doing.'

'Explain to me, Doctor,' Guena said. 'What is the harm in using these things?'

'And explain quickly,' I said. 'These passages are well concealed, but Conrad's men will be searching the palace thoroughly for Guena and myself.'

The Doctor took out the thin metal wand that he carried everywhere with him. 'I've been monitoring what happens whenever anyone uses one of these things,' he said. 'The lights, the swords, the mirrors, the water. Not good. Draws a lot of power. And the power is drawn from the land itself. Your ancestors knew what they were doing – more or less. Even so, they overreached themselves. Used their clever gadgets too much. Built too many; built too ambitiously. Flew to the stars – although I don't think they got past your system. Anyway, that's what caused their decline. But they left you with all these things lying around, like children picking up guns and playing with them, thinking that they're just toys that go whizz and bang. But they're not toys. They're dangerous. Really dangerous.'

I thought that I was beginning to understand. 'The sickness in the countryside,' I said. 'The wastes and the ruins. The people – all gone.'

'People knew that the land was sick. That there was no future in Varuz. And there couldn't be – not as long as the nobles kept on using these devices that they barely understood.' He looked at Guena.

'Every time you lit your halls, every time you drew your swords, every time you spoke to each other through them – you were killing a little more of Varuz. This stuff was your ruin.'

My lady stood with her head bowed. 'We thought we were keeping to the old ways—'

'And you were,' said the Doctor, 'but you didn't really understand.'

Slowly, Guena began to take off her rings, one by one, piling them in a little heap upon the ground. Her necklace followed, and her brooches and then, last of all, she tore the jewel-encrusted sleeves from her dress and left them piled by the rest. 'If that is the case, then let us leave it all behind then. Let Conrad destroy the lot.'

I loved her more at that moment than I had ever done. How easy it would have been at that time to cling to anything that gave her power. But it was not worth this price.

'He will, Guena,' the Doctor said. 'And so he should, because otherwise they'll kill him and his people too. Conrad is a clever man, and he surrounds himself with clever people. If they want lights – they'll make lights. If they want heating – they'll make heating. But they won't pick up someone else's toys. They'll make their own.'

'What about Clara?' I said. 'How will we find her now?'

The Doctor smiled. 'I've got my own ways of finding Clara.' He opened the door to the box. 'Step inside,' he said. 'I've got something truly marvellous to show you.'

Alone on the hillside, blinking back tears, Clara watched the battle rage. The day wore on and the shadows lengthened, and, as the sun began to set, one of the buildings near the gates caught fire. There was no one to stop it, and soon the blaze had spread across the whole city. Clara thought of the halls she had seen, that even in their decline had managed to be beautiful. All burning. She rubbed her eyes, and her hands came away damp with tears. Then, as night fell, she heard a familiar, heartening sound.

The TARDIS.

Once it had completely materialised, the Doctor emerged, looking pensive, and, behind him, looking dazed, came Guena and Bernhardt.

Clara recognised that look. 'You know what I've said, Doctor,' she said, trying to keep her voice cheerful. 'You can't go around showing people infinity. They get scared.'

Bernhardt turned to look at the city. Taking

Guena's hand, the two of them stood, watching the fire take their home.

'I'm sorry,' said Clara. Slowly, she removed the pendant from around her neck. 'Here,' she said, offering it to Guena. 'You should take this. Something saved from the ruins.'

She was surprised when Guena pulled away. 'Those days are gone,' she said. 'And they must not return. I will not ask you to keep that in memory of me, Clara, because I am not sure it would turn out well for you.' She glanced at the Doctor, who shook his head. 'Bury it,' she said. 'Or break it. But do not take it with you.'

'Doctor,' said Clara, uncertainly. 'What's this all about?'

'All those pretty toys,' said the Doctor. 'Turns out they weren't so safe after all.'

'Death rays, huh?'

'Something like that,' the Doctor said.

As he was speaking, Clara felt the jewel warm in her hand. 'Doctor,' she said, holding it out in front of her. 'Someone's trying to contact me.'

On the stream, an image was trying to form.

'What should I do?' Clara said. 'Should I chuck it in the river?'

'No, wait,' said the Doctor. 'I think this is someone I need to speak to, before we go.'

'Mikhail,' whispered Guena, as the young man's face took shape and form.

'Aunt,' he said. 'Have you gone?'

'Aye,' she said.

'Good. I sent them to the north wing in the hope you would go the other way.'

'Am I to thank you for your mercy, Mikhail?' she said proudly.

'No,' he said. 'I do not want your thanks. You did what you thought was best for me, throughout our lives together. I am grateful for that. I have no wish to see you dead. But you – and Bernhardt – should leave Varuz as quickly as you can. Conrad will be looking for you, and he will not show mercy.'

'Mikhail,' said the Doctor. 'Listen to me. This is very important.' Quickly, he explained his discovery: that the devices handed down by their ancestors were what had caused the decline of Varuz, and were what was making the land sicken. 'You need to destroy this stuff – and quickly. Don't use it again. I don't think it's reached the point of no return, but it might be soon.'

Mikhail listened to his story carefully. 'I understand, Doctor,' he said. 'And I think that Conrad and his men will perform this task gratefully. Thank you for your warning.' Mikhail spoke to Guena and Bernhardt once again. 'Good luck, Aunt, wherever your road now takes you. And to you, too, Lord Bernhardt. I think you have achieved your heart's desire – and a just reward.' Then Mikhail smiled at Clara. 'Goodbye, lady. Remember us.'

And then he was gone. The Doctor turned to Guena and Bernhardt, eyeing the pair thoughtfully. 'So what are you going to do?' he said. 'You can't go back down there. Conrad will know that you've escaped, Guena, and he'll suspect you're involved, Bernhardt. They'll be hunting for you.'

'Don't say it like you're relishing it, Doctor,' said Clara. 'Can't we help, somehow?'

'I'm not getting into a civil war, Clara, if that's what you're asking.'

'No more war,' said Bernhardt. 'And what would we fight for? The country that we loved was not what we thought. I would not restore it, knowing what I know now.'

The Doctor looked at Guena. 'And you, Duchess? Are you happy for this to be the end?'

Guena was watching the fire as it burned brightly. 'Happy? Of course not. But…' She gave a deep sigh. 'Bernhardt is right. That is not a kind of rule that I desire.'

Bernhardt reached out and took her hand. 'My lady,' he said. 'Beloved. We can make a new life for ourselves.'

'Where would we go?' she said. 'There is nowhere now that does not belong to Conrad.'

'But the world has many quiet corners,' he insisted. 'We can find a home, you and I.'

'You can't cross the mountains,' said the Doctor. 'The soldiers would find you. But I can take you across the border. Set you on your way.'

They accepted the offer gratefully and, in the middle of the night, had you been out on a quiet lane, in a quiet corner of the quietest part in Conrad's great country, you might have seen a strange dark box appear from nowhere, and four people emerge. Two would stay, and two would go on their way: a pair of pilgrims, on their way to a distant shrine.

Clara had not wanted to return to the city, but the Doctor insisted, saying that he wanted to be sure that Mikhail had listened.

And it seemed he had: Conrad's men were busy, gathering up all they could find in the palace, and throwing their collections onto the fire.

The Doctor and Clara stood near one small bonfire and listened to the people talking to each other. 'Sorceries,' she heard one woman say to another. 'The nobles kept it all to themselves anyway. But Conrad's people will bring new machines and new ideas. Maybe better days are coming now.'

Clara took the pendant and threw it on the fire.

Later, the townsfolk gathered in the main square, and Mikhail came to speak to them: the young lord; the heir of their old Duke. 'I know this seems an unhappy time,' he said, 'but we have turned the corner now. The darkest days are over. The land, and the country, will start to get better now. I shall not be here as much as I would like, but I will be here when I can. And I will always speak for you. This country is my home – the land between the mountains and the sea.'

The Doctor took Clara by the arm. 'Come on,' he said. 'The future's safe – or as safe as it can ever be.'

And they stole away into the darkness.

'Was that really Lancelot?' Clara said, later, when they were back in the TARDIS.

'Clara…'

'Yes, yes, he didn't exist, but…' She shivered, remembering that ancient knight, sitting in grim silence in the dark. 'He seemed real enough to me.'

The Doctor stood before the console, contemplating infinity. 'There's room in the universe for many wonders,' he said. 'And stories must have sources. Arthur lived, that much is true. So perhaps those knights did come to Earth once upon a time. Perhaps they did pass through his court, when the old order was crumbling and the records turning to dust, already centuries into their quest, chasing a treasure they were carrying with them all along. And so they continue…' He punched the controls. 'I can only hope, Clara, that one day they can remember who they are, and rest.'

The TARDIS dematerialised. And the Quest went on.

I am the last, unless those strange wanderers who passed through Varuz in those last days remember something of us yet. But when I think of them, and reflect upon them, it seems to me that were cloaked in a kind of deliberate forgetfulness, as if their pasts were not to be admitted, keeping them mindful of nothing more than the present… Do they remember us? Do they remember me? Do they remember Varuz?

Acknowledgements

Thank you to Albert DePetrillo, Justin Richards, and Steve Tribe for their help in writing in this book.

My grateful thanks and love to Matthew, who gives me the space and time to be able to both write and be Mummy. And love to Verity, who likes Daleks.

BBC
DOCTOR WHO
Big Bang Generation
Gary Russell

ISBN 978-1-101-90581-4

I'm an archaeologist, but probably not the one you were expecting.

Christmas 2015, Sydney, New South Wales, Australia

Imagine everyone's surprise when a time portal opens up in Sydney Cove. Imagine their shock as a massive pyramid now sits beside the Harbour Bridge, inconveniently blocking Port Jackson and glowing with energy. Imagine their fear as Cyrrus 'the mobster' Globb, Professor Horace Jaanson and an alien assassin called Kik arrive to claim the glowing pyramid. Finally imagine everyone's dismay when they are followed by a bunch of con artists out to spring their greatest grift yet.

This gang consists of Legs (the sexy comedian), Dog Boy (providing protection and firepower), Shortie (handling logistics), Da Trowel (in charge of excavation and history) and their leader, Doc (busy making sure the universe isn't destroyed in an explosion that makes the Big Bang look like a damp squib).

And when someone accidentally reawakens the Ancients of Time – which, Doc reckons, wasn't the wisest or best-judged of actions – things get a whole lot more complicated…

An original novel featuring the Twelfth Doctor, as played by Peter Capaldi